"I know you're in there, Joslyn," the man said through the door.

"We have Clay. Give yourself up and we won't hurt him."

She only had to stall them until the police arrived. But what if they killed Clay before that happened?

Then Clay's voice sounded from behind the back door, "She's not in there. I came alone." They must have dragged him to the backyard, where there were fewer people to see.

"I know you're lying," the man said calmly to Clay.

Then Clay's voice shot out in a cry of pain.

Joslyn forced herself to breathe, to relax. She had to stay calm, stay focused.

"Joslyn, come out or we'll send Clay here to his stepdaddy in little pieces."

Moving quietly and staying low, Joslyn crept from behind the table until she was behind the sink. She slowly rose until she could see outside the window that hung right over the sink.

The man shouted, "Joslyn, you come out right now, or I swear I'll—"

Suddenly Clay snapped his head backward and clocked his captor full in the face. The man grunted, and Clay pulled free.

A gun went off.

Camy Tang grew up in Hawaii and now lives in northern California with her engineer husband and rambunctious dog. She graduated from Stanford University and was a biologist researcher, but now she writes full-time. She is a staff worker for her church youth group and leads one of the Sunday worship teams. Visit camytang.com to read free short stories and subscribe to her email newsletter.

Books by Camy Tang

Love Inspired Suspense

Deadly Intent
Formula for Danger
Stalker in the Shadows
Narrow Escape
Treacherous Intent
Gone Missing

Visit the Author Profile page at Harlequin.com for more titles

GONE MISSING

CAMY TANG

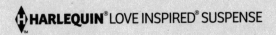

HARLEQUIN® LOVE INSPIRED® SUSPENSE

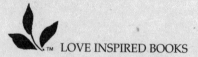

Recycling programs
for this product may
not exist in your area.

LOVE INSPIRED BOOKS

ISBN-13: 978-0-373-67679-8

Gone Missing

www.Harlequin.com

Printed in U.S.A.

Above all, love each other deeply,
because love covers over a multitude of sins.
—*1 Peter* 4:8

For my grandmother, who showed me
what it was to be a strong woman. I will miss you.

ONE

The man had danger written all over him.

Or maybe that was just Joslyn's perception because of the grim cast to his mouth and the way his powerful body moved with the athletic grace of a man confident in his physical strength. His blue-gray eyes found hers across the hot sidewalk in front of Fiona Crowley's Phoenix home, and her vision wavered as if he were a mirage.

The sun glinted off of the straight, blond-streaked, brown hair that fell over his forehead, and it triggered a memory for her. Fiona had the same hair color, and in pictures she'd shown Joslyn of her brother, they'd looked very much alike.

Joslyn looked more closely at the man as he closed the car door and approached her where she stood at the edge of Fiona's front yard. He had golden-brown stubble that softened his square jaw, but there was no doubt that the shape of his face was the same as Fiona's, although wider and more sharply cut.

"Are you…Clay?" Joslyn guessed as he stopped in front of her.

His low brow wrinkled. "Who are you?" His voice was deep but not gravelly, with a smoothness that made her think of honey.

The Arizona sun had been unbearably hot since six this morning, but it suddenly became a furnace. A bead of sweat trickled down the side of her neck, and she wiped at it. "I'm Joslyn Dimalanta. I was good friends with Fiona when she lived in Los Angeles—we were classmates in the same master's degree program. You're her brother, right? You look exactly like her."

"Half brother." There was a tinge of bitterness in his tone. "What are you doing here?"

"I'm here looking for Fiona." She straightened her shoulders. "I got a postcard from her—"

"When?" Clay's eyes suddenly became more intense, and he took a half step toward her.

He wasn't a large man, but something about the strength simmering beneath his wide shoulders gave Joslyn a flash of memory of her abusive ex-boyfriend, and her heartbeat went into red alert for a second. It must have showed on her face, because he looked conscientious and quickly stepped back.

She took a long breath before answering him. "Fiona sent it three weeks ago, but I only got it a few days ago. It was sent to my old address in LA."

"Three weeks? I got a phone call from her three weeks ago."

"What did she say? Is she all right?"

"She said, 'Clay, help me,' and then she hung up." A muscle flexed in his jaw.

"Did she sound frightened? Stressed?"

"Her voice shook." Worry was etched in his face, in the lines between his brows and alongside his mouth. "I hadn't heard from her in..." He stopped himself and looked away.

Joslyn knew, from what Fiona had mentioned back in LA, that Fiona and Clay had been close as children, but had drifted apart. "Before I got the postcard, I hadn't spoken to Fiona in the two years since she left LA." Why would she reach out to him now?

"What did she say?"

"She said she was in trouble and needed my help. But she didn't say where she was." The handwriting had been messy, as if written in a hurry, but she'd recognized it as Fiona's.

"Where was the postmark from?"

"Phoenix. The card was a touristy Grand Canyon design, prestamped."

Clay frowned. "That's strange. Why would she call me and send you a postcard?"

And why wouldn't she say anything more than that she needed help? The knot at the base of her skull tightened even more. "It's why I came here. I had to do some digging to find her address—

after she left LA, it looks like she didn't want to be found."

"I had to hire a private investigator to find this address for me." But there was uncertainty in his face as he glanced at the house. The house's large front bay window had white curtains pulled across it, and there was no way to know if anyone was inside. "Did you ring the doorbell?"

"No, I just got here."

Clay's mouth was grim. "Maybe it was just a bad joke."

On two people Fiona hadn't spoken to in years? Joslyn didn't think it was likely, but the alternative was that Fiona was in serious trouble.

Clay strode up the concrete walkway that wound through the stone garden in the front yard to the door. "Let's hope she doesn't run away screaming when she sees me," he muttered.

"Fiona always talked about what a great big brother you were," Joslyn said. Protective. Someone she'd trust. Fiona had loved him dearly, but had simply shaken her head sadly when Joslyn asked why she didn't try to get in touch with Clay again after all these years.

He looked at Joslyn in surprise, his eyes lightening to blue. It transformed his serious face into that of a man from whom a great burden had been lifted. But then pain flickered across his gaze and he turned away.

Joslyn followed him to the front door, trying to

wrap her head around everything that had come out in the past few minutes. This was too much thrown at her at once—not just Fiona's postcard, but her phone call to Clay, equally as vague. And then meeting Clay here, seeing firsthand the strength in his body and the fearless way he carried himself, fitting the stories Fiona had told Joslyn about Clay being a mob strong-arm in Chicago, before he went to prison.

Her first reaction had been attraction, but her second had been wariness. She'd suffered physically and emotionally at the hands of her ex-boyfriend. She knew that not all strong men would hurt her, but she had become extra cautious about making herself vulnerable again.

Clay rang the doorbell, and they could faintly hear it ding-dong inside the house. He stood with his hands in his jeans pockets, but there was a tension across his wide shoulders that belied his casual pose. He rang the doorbell again. Still no answer.

Joslyn checked her watch. It was eight o'clock on Monday morning. "Maybe she went to work already."

"Do you know where she works?"

"She's IT support at a manufacturing company." It was a rather low-paying job for Fiona, assuming she'd ended up finally getting her degree, but maybe she couldn't get anything on a higher pay scale, or maybe she preferred the hours there.

Clay's eyes narrowed to a stormy gray. "You said you haven't talked to her in two years. How do you know all this?"

"It's my job to find out stuff like this. I'm training to be a skip tracer."

"A skip tracer?"

"I find people. I also help people disappear." Joslyn had been especially grateful to her friend Elisabeth, who had originally helped her escape her abusive ex, a Filipino gang captain in Los Angeles. Elisabeth had gotten Joslyn a job in the O'Neill Agency while she finished her last few quarters of school. Joslyn found she enjoyed helping people, especially other women who wanted to get away from dangerous relationships. She understood their situations only too well and only hoped that Fiona wasn't suffering at the hands of a man.

Clay went to the front window to try to peer through the crack in the curtains. Joslyn noticed an envelope sticking out of the mail box next to the door and opened the lid. It was full of mail. It didn't look as though Fiona got a lot of junk mail, but some envelopes she did get were postmarked several weeks ago. "I don't think Fiona's been home for a while." A chill crept over her skin.

Clay frowned. "I don't like this."

"I know where Fiona usually kept a spare key," Joslyn said. "In the back, under—"

"The ugliest gnome," Clay finished for her,

flashing a smile. His eyes crinkled and turned a glittering aquamarine, and Joslyn's heartbeat blipped. While Fiona was beautiful, her brother was incredibly handsome.

"How do you know that?" she asked.

"She got that from me. It's where I hid the spare key at my house back in Chicago, years ago."

They headed around the side of the house, through the wooden latch gate, which was unlocked. The shade from the building made the temperature drop a few degrees, but it was still oppressively hot.

The backyard was small and bricked over, with plant beds along the walls containing a few orange and lemon trees. However, there was also a line of little gnome statues next to the glass back door, and the ugliest one was clearly the largest, a hideous creature with a long nose and a grinning mouth full of grimy teeth. Clay tipped it over and found a key underneath.

Joslyn tried to peer through the wooden slats of the blinds covering the glass door, but couldn't see anything in the darkened room beyond except for a glimpse of a television set and a leather couch. The space seemed unusually dark considering the number of windows the house had.

Clay inserted the key and it turned smoothly. He swung the handle and eased the door open.

Then suddenly he was grabbing her and leaping aside just as an explosion shattered the morning.

* * *

The noise of the blast boomed in Clay's ears as he rolled with Joslyn, protecting her with his body. The heat from the blast rushed over his back like an ocean wave, and debris pelted them like hail.

His brain felt like a bottle of soda that had been shaken and popped open, with fizzing bubbles clouding his vision. A ringing roared in his ears, dominating all other sound. He blinked, and his vision cleared to the sight of Joslyn's dark hair tumbled over the bricks of the yard. He was sprawled on top of her, and he could smell apricot and jasmine, and the scent of walking through a quiet wood.

"Are you all right?" His voice came from far away. He rolled to the side so he wasn't crushing her beneath him. "Joslyn?"

She moved slowly, lifting her head. Her clear, golden-brown eyes were dazed. She didn't speak, but simply looked at him in confusion.

"Anything broken?"

She slowly sat up, checking her slender limbs. She shook her head, then looked behind him at the house.

There was a gaping hole where the back door had been. Plaster from the exploded wall still rained from the air. The roof lurched drunkenly.

"Come on, we need to get clear of the house." He rose to his feet, feeling aches in his joints from the blast and the hard landing on the bricks. Joslyn took the hand he held out to her, and they skirted around the less damaged side of the house to get to the front again.

Fiona's next-door neighbor had rushed out to her front yard, an older woman with gray, permed hair, dressed in a tank top and shorts. She gaped at them as they appeared. "Are you all right? What happened? Good gracious, was that a bomb? Fiona's poor house. What was a bomb doing in her house?"

What *was* a bomb doing in Fiona's house? It had been rigged to explode as soon as the door was breached. Clay had been incredibly lucky to see the tripwire as he opened the door, and his reflexes had taken over, allowing him to grab Joslyn and leap to safety. Luckily, it looked as if it hadn't been a very large explosion, although it had been enough to blow out a few of the windows in the house. Glass covered the stone garden in the front yard.

Clay was starting to recover his hearing because he now heard a dog barking from inside the house next door and a car alarm sounding from somewhere nearby. Luckily, there hadn't been many people home at this time of morning on this street—just the next-door neighbor, and a couple people from houses across the street, including one older woman with two young children.

"We need to call the police," Joslyn said to the neighbor.

Clay's shoulders knotted. Once the police realized he was an ex-convict at the site of an explosion, things would get interesting. This had nothing to do with his past.

At least, he hoped it didn't. The mob family he'd worked for years ago, before he'd gone to prison, was now defunct, and he hadn't been very high on the totem pole to begin with. He didn't think he had any enemies left who would want revenge on him, but if he did, then rigging his sister's house to blow up was a rather melodramatic way to do it. A sniper shot would have been easier.

"I'm calling them right now," said a neighbor from across the street who had her cell phone. "I can't believe this. My great-grandkids are with me today, too."

The two kids were standing in the street staring wide-eyed at the house, which didn't look much different from the front except for some dust and curls of smoke rising from the broken windows. "Can we go see—"

"No," their great-grandmother said firmly, then spoke into the phone as the police dispatcher picked up the line. "Yes, I'm here at Braeden Court, and there's been an explosion!" She gave Clay a suspicious look.

"Oh, don't mind her," Fiona's next-door neighbor said to Clay. "She thinks the government put microchips in polio vaccines so they could monitor everyone." The woman waved a finger in a circle around her ear. "Completely cuckoo."

"Are you all right?" Joslyn asked her. "Your house is right next door."

"Luckily there's a lot of space in the side yards and the fence is good and thick. My windows rattled but no damage. I'm Mary, by the way." She held out a gnarled hand.

Joslyn and Clay introduced themselves, and Mary looked closely at Clay. "You related to Fiona? You look just like her."

"She's my half sister."

"I'm a friend of hers from Los Angeles," Joslyn said. "We came here to see her."

Mary's steel-gray eyebrows rose. "I'd hoped she'd just gone to visit someone like one of you when she disappeared."

"She disappeared?" Clay had to fight the alarm he felt.

"A few weeks ago, I heard barking from her house and went to see what was going on. She gave me a spare key because sometimes she asks me to take care of her dog, Poochie. Looked like the poor thing had been left alone for a day or two, so I took him." Mary jabbed a thumb backward toward her house, where the dog was still barking intermittently. "I haven't seen any sign of Fiona since. I filed a police report, but they haven't done anything. Do you think her vanishing has something to do with the blast? Thank God it didn't happen when I got her dog." Mary shuddered at the close call. "Was it a gas leak or something?"

"Um…we're not sure," Joslyn said carefully. She looked briefly at Clay, but he somehow knew what she was thinking. The less they told the neighbors, the better.

"We were opening the door when it blew up," Clay said to Mary.

"My goodness, are you two all right? You don't look injured, but…"

"We're fine," Joslyn said.

"You better make sure you get seen by a doctor," Mary said.

"What happened?" People started to arrive from other streets in the area, gaping at the house. Mary was only too happy to tell them a dramatized account of the explosion.

Clay pulled Joslyn aside. "You sure you're okay?" he asked her. She was tall but slender, and she seemed so delicate.

She nodded, although there was worry in her face. "Who rigged Fiona's house to explode?"

"Your guess is as good as mine. But whoever did it is a ruthless killer." He sighed and eyed the ruined shell of the house.

Joslyn shivered, even in the sweltering heat.

Clay had dealt with men just as ruthless when

he'd been a street thug for that mob family in Chicago. He hadn't killed anyone, but if he'd kept going down that road, who knows what he might have become?

That thought was like a dark blot on his soul.

Police sirens blared, and soon a squad car turned the corner and barreled down the street toward them, followed by paramedics. Clay's shoulders tensed out of habit, and he relaxed them. He wondered if there would ever be a time when his past wouldn't crop up in his present.

He answered the officers' questions evenly, but that only seemed to make them suspicious, if the curious looks they threw at him were any indication. He submitted to the paramedic's exam, but other than a few minor cuts from flying glass and debris, he was unhurt. Part of the door frame had hit him on the side and a chunk of plaster had glanced off his shoulder, but he shook off the bruises. He'd had worse.

He knew the exact moment the officers had looked him up and found out about his prison record. They had hard glints in their eyes as they approached him. "So Mr. Ashton, what are you doing here in Arizona? You're a long ways from Illinois." The officer's name badge read Campbell.

"I came to see my half sister, Fiona Crowley."

"And that's it, huh?" Officer Talbot, the younger man, squinted up at him. "Nothing else?"

"Nothing else," Clay said through a tight jaw. He might have been tempted to mention the phone call from his sister if it hadn't been for the suspicion in their tones. Anything he said to them would only make things worse for himself, and he needed to be able to find Fiona and make sure she was safe.

"So you just opened the door and the house exploded? Kind of odd, don't you think?"

"It might have been a gas leak or something like that."

"You didn't have anything to do with it?" Officer Talbot gave him a look that said, *Yeah, right.*

"I had nothing to do with this." His voice came out a bit harsher than he intended.

"And Miss Dima…Dia…" Officer Talbot squinted at his notebook. "What's your *relationship* with her?"

Clay gritted his teeth. "I just met Joslyn when we both arrived at the house at the same time. To see Fiona. Why is it that the police didn't contact me, *her brother*, when her neighbor filed a missing persons report?"

Officer Talbot's face turned pink and he glanced at his partner. "It's under investigation," he snapped.

Calm down. Clay had to calm down. His temper had gotten him in enough trouble in the past. He couldn't afford to get in trouble now, when Fiona might be in danger. He wanted to walk away from these two men and the insulting ring to their questions, but he forced himself to stand in a relaxed stance.

Officer Campbell gave him a hard look, but then he said, "We have your hotel information and phone number. We'll be in touch." It was almost like a threat. However, the two men turned and left him. They began addressing the other people gathered on the sidewalk.

Joslyn came up to him, but paused when she saw his face.

"They were giving you a hard time?"

"Nothing unexpected." Considering his prison time. But it still bothered him.

Her eyes sparked amber. "But you were visiting your *sister*."

"Look, I don't know how much Fiona told you—"

"She knew about your time in prison," Joslyn said quietly.

"Well, it's not something officers of the law can forget about."

"I suppose you're right, but you didn't have anything to do with this."

"They don't know that."

She sighed and looked away. He could almost hear her thoughts. She knew he was right. "Mary was able to give me the exact date she went to collect Poochie. Fiona's been gone for three weeks, about the time of the stamp on the postcard she sent me."

Clay frowned. "I just can't imagine where she would go. Why did she need to leave? Is she really in trouble?" He wondered if it was even Fiona who'd reached out to him and Joslyn.

"I was going to drop by her workplace. Since it looks like Fiona doesn't want to be found, I want to gather as much information as I can about her life here in Phoenix to try to predict where she'd go." Joslyn eyed the officers. Talbot was flirting with a young woman, while Campbell was speaking to two men in business-casual clothing. "They say, out of sight out of mind, so did you want to come with me?"

Maybe the less the cops saw of him, the less likely they would be to blame him for the explosion. "Sure." Right now, it was the only lead they had on where Fiona might be. After that explosion, he had a feeling this wasn't a case of his sister going on a spontaneous vacation. He'd been worried before, but now his fear for her was like a boiling pot in his gut.

If there was something dangerous going on, he wanted to make sure he was there to face it head-on.

TWO

"We're being followed," Clay said, looking in the rearview mirror.

"Are you sure?" Joslyn angled herself so she could get a better look behind them through the passenger-side mirror, but all she saw were several white cars, a couple minivans, an SUV.

"The white Taurus, about four cars behind us."

Joslyn tried to get a look at it, but could only see half of the blurry face of the man in the passenger seat of the Taurus. Still, the brief glimpse made her heart race.

"Do you recognize him?" Clay asked.

"No."

"Me, neither."

"How long have they been following us?"

"I didn't see them on the way to Fiona's workplace, but they appeared behind us when we started for the museum."

They'd gone to the air-conditioning parts manufacturer Fiona worked for, only to hear that three weeks ago, a man had called, claiming to be her brother, asking for extended leave for her, citing a family emergency. However, the manager hadn't been able to get in touch with her after that and she'd been fired.

Who had called? It obviously wasn't Clay. That may be why the police hadn't followed up on the missing person's report—if they checked with Fiona's company, the manager had heard from her and so there wasn't a problem, at least at the time Mary notified them of her disappearance.

Perhaps that had been the point of calling in to Fiona's workplace—to forestall the filing of the report. Joslyn and Clay had exchanged tense looks. Did someone have Fiona?

They'd spoken to a couple of her coworkers who had been outside for a smoke break, but they hadn't learned much—Fiona apparently wasn't close with anyone at work, even though she'd been working there about fifteen months. It had seemed like a dead end.

But Joslyn remembered that Fiona often visited art museums in Los Angeles. She'd been friends with the guards at the museum and had formed friendships with other people who visited the museum regularly, mostly artists and critics. Clay had agreed that she'd done the same in Chicago, when she had lived with him in the years during college and after she'd graduated. So they'd left Joslyn's car in the business parking lot and headed to the largest art museum in Phoenix, the Kevin Tran Museum of Art and Art History.

But they apparently weren't alone.

Were their pursuers aiming to finish the job, since the explosion at Fiona's house hadn't gotten rid of them, or did they simply want to question Joslyn and Clay? "I wonder if they want to stop us from finding Fiona, or if they think we know where she is," Joslyn said.

"It probably wouldn't be a good idea to stop and ask them." Clay signaled and switched lanes.

Joslyn had been in this exact situation barely a year ago, running from her ex-boyfriend, nervously looking behind her to make sure she wasn't followed. Feeling as if her life wasn't her own anymore. She had thought she'd put those days behind her, yet here she was again. "Phoenix is a grid. How are you going to lose them?"

"I have to get onto a freeway."

He got onto the 101 almost casually, as if he'd always meant to head in that direction, and moved into the leftmost lane. He then slowed down, and soon the white Taurus was directly behind them. Clay was driving so slowly in the fast lane that cars were passing them on the right, and the Taurus couldn't stay hidden. There were two men in the sedan, both with sunglasses on. The shorter one had curly, dark hair, while the other had close-cropped, dark hair. They also both had identical frowns.

"They know you're on to them," she said.

"It won't matter in a moment. Hang on." He cranked the wheel hard to the right and cut off an SUV. Its driver honked at them as Clay swerved right again and cut off a Toyota. He then zoomed right in front of a Mustang in the freeway exit lane only a few feet before it split from the highway, separated by a concrete divider. Joslyn knew the circumstances were extreme, but the sight of the cars looming so close in front of them made her heart shoot up to her throat.

His aggressive driving had carried them too quickly across the lanes for the Taurus to keep up. The driver couldn't make it to the right hand lane in time to exit, and Joslyn saw both men glaring at them as they were forced to continue on the freeway.

"You lost them." Joslyn had always been rather cautious behind the wheel, trying not to annoy anyone around her. Clay had cut off three cars in fewer than three seconds.

"Not yet." Clay wove his way through the traffic and began driving in random circles.

He was a good driver, his motions controlled and precise, the car moving smoothly, almost effortlessly through traffic. But there was tension radiating from the corners of his eyes as he glanced in his rearview mirrors.

Joslyn kept an eye out behind them, also, and her heartbeat continued to gallop in her chest as she waited to see if the white Taurus or some other car would suddenly appear. But after several miles, she never saw the same car twice.

Clay finally nodded. "I think we did lose them."

"How did they find us? Why are they following us?" She didn't like not knowing. "Are you sure they followed us from her workplace?"

"They could have followed us from her house and we just didn't see them," Clay said. "Although I don't like the thought that they were watching us the entire time."

"I don't, either." It made her feel vulnerable, right when she had been working so hard to get back control in her life.

Clay's mouth grew hard. "Maybe they were the ones who rigged her house to explode and they were waiting to see who would show up."

For a moment, he looked so much like her ex-boyfriend that Joslyn had to look away. Tomas had hated being trapped by other men, and it had brought out an ugly side of him. He'd had many ugly sides.

She took a deep breath. That chapter in her life was over. Tomas was in jail. She was safe. She had been doing everything in her power to make sure she stayed safe.

Except that it hadn't saved her from walking into this situation. "If they did rig her house to explode, they either wanted to kill her or anyone after her."

"I don't think anyone would expend manpower to watch an empty house for weeks, just to make sure the explosion killed someone looking for Fiona," Clay said. "*If* they were staking out the house, it's because they want to find Fiona, dead or alive."

"So Fiona might be alive. On the run."

"Let's hope so. But if those men weren't staking out the house already, it could mean they followed one of us to Fiona's house."

Joslyn thought back to what she'd had to do to find Fiona's address. Had her digging around alerted someone that she was after Fiona? But who? What in the world had Fiona gotten into? "Did you have any idea Fiona was in serious trouble like this?" Joslyn asked.

He shook his head slowly. "I hadn't talked to her in years. I didn't even know where she'd gone after she left Chicago. I tried to find her but then..."

He'd gone to prison. Joslyn wondered why Fiona hadn't reached out to him, especially when it seemed that he still loved her. Fiona hadn't indicated there had been any bad blood or grudges between them, so why hadn't she wanted to see her brother again?

"I didn't know, either," Joslyn said. "Fiona was just like any other girl when I knew her in Los Angeles, going to classes, hanging out with friends. Except..." She thought back. "She seemed a little sad sometimes, but I knew her mother had died and she didn't like to talk about her father. I thought she just missed her mom."

"She and Mom were close," Clay said quietly.

"I still can't get over the job she got here in Phoenix. She was qualified for a position that paid so much more."

"She must have gotten into some kind of trouble, something that made her need to take a different job than she normally would have."

"She didn't have many friends at her workplace, so maybe the answer isn't in her job, but in what she did outside her job." Which meant that if she did visit the museum here, as she had done in Los Angeles and Chicago, they might find something about what she'd been involved in. A standard tactic for skip tracers was to find out as much about the person as possible to figure out where they'd go.

The Kevin Tran Museum of Art and Art History was a beautiful sandstone building that rose out of the desert like a castle, surrounded by artfully arranged rock formations and different types of cacti. As they paid the entrance fee, Joslyn grabbed a pamphlet about becoming a season pass holder or a museum patron.

"If I'm right, Fiona would have gotten at least a season pass for the museum. She had a season ticket for one of the museums in Los Angeles that she enjoyed going to. She got invited to private showings and a few art galas."

"She had a season pass for one of the museums in Chicago, too," Clay said. "She took me to an art opening once. I had to wear a suit." He grinned, suddenly. "She told me I looked like a bouncer." But then something, some memory, made the light dim from his eyes and his smile. Joslyn had to stop herself from asking him what had made him so sad.

She consulted the pamphlet and saw that the patron services department was in charge of handling business with season pass holders. "This way." There were signs pointing the way to the patron services office.

They passed through several galleries. Some had ethnic themes, such as one long room with art from several premier Chinese American artists who had first settled in Phoenix at the turn of the century, and another room with huge murals of Native American art. One gallery housed a display of sculptures that looked like they were made from desert rocks of various colors.

"This is a museum Fiona would love," Clay said as they crossed a room where Native American woven blankets hung from the walls. "She always talked about how art can tell you all about different cultures and periods of history."

"I have to admit I didn't always see it," Joslyn said. "But then again, when Fiona went with me to a concert, she didn't go into raptures about the musical nuances the way I did."

"What kind of concerts?"

Out of habit, Joslyn hesitated before answering. "Mostly classical music. Fiona was my only friend who'd go to concerts with me and not fall asleep in the middle."

"I like classic rock, myself. But I've been known to listen to some instrumental movie scores, too."

She blinked at him, then laughed. "The classic rock I would have guessed."

His smile was open and charming. "Don't judge a book by its cover."

It would be so easy to fall for that charm. But then again, Tomas had been charming, too, at first.

They arrived at a door marked "Patron Services" and went inside. A woman sat behind a desk with horn-rimmed glasses and smiled at them. "May I help you?" Her name plaque read Ruby Padalecki.

Joslyn gave her one of her new business cards. "I'm an investigator with the O'Neill Agency. We're looking into the disappearance of a young woman who might have been a season pass holder with the museum, Fiona Crowley."

Ruby's mouth grew pinched. "I'm afraid I can't give any information about our museum patrons."

"We're just worried about her," Clay said. "I'm her brother."

The woman looked at him with her brow furrowed. "Oh, my, you look exactly like…" She swallowed and lowered her voice. "I'm sorry, but I could lose my job."

"No, we don't want you to do anything to jeopardize that," Joslyn said quickly.

Clay held his hands up. "We're just museum patrons chatting with you, okay? We're not after any confidential information that might get you in trouble."

Ruby relaxed and smiled. "Okay, sure."

He looked harmless, approachable. She envied the easy way he could engage with Ruby. Joslyn always felt awkward socially. It was the reason she liked computers so much.

Clay leaned a hip against the edge of the desk. "My sister likes visiting art museums. She visited all the ones in Chicago."

"She also liked visiting museums when I knew her in Los Angeles," Joslyn said.

Ruby nodded. "Oh, she comes in here every week. Sometimes a few times a week."

"Once, a museum had a new exhibit by a well-known artist and she went five times that week," Joslyn said. "I began to wonder if she was in love with the artist until I found out he was sixty-five years old."

"There was one artist in Chicago who was

twenty-five," Clay said dryly. "I was a little worried since she was only seventeen at the time."

"What did you do about that?" Ruby asked.

Clay scratched the back of his head. "I have to admit, I was really mean. I was at some party with her, and I went to where she was talking to the artist. I told him an embarrassing story about when she was in kindergarten that involved feathers, glitter and pink panties. She didn't speak to me for a week, but she didn't talk to the artist again, so it was a win for me."

Joslyn and Ruby laughed. "She actually told me that story," Ruby told him, "so she must have gotten over it."

"No artists here that she's currently in love with?" Clay said.

Ruby winced. "Well, there is one Native American artist who's tall, dark and swarthy—he looks like a pirate. All the girls on staff here think he's incredibly handsome. Fiona's friendly with him, but then again, she's just as friendly with Rufus, one of the guards."

Clay cleared his throat. "How often is the, uh, artist here?"

Ruby giggled. "Not very often. Don't worry."

"When's the last time you talked to Fiona?" Joslyn asked.

Ruby sobered. "It's been several weeks. Rufus and I are a little worried. I even called her house a few times, but she didn't answer."

"Why do you think she'd stop coming to the museum?" Clay asked.

"Rufus thinks it's because of that man who came a few weeks ago."

"What man?"

"Some older man talked to her in the ancient Chinese art room. You should talk to Rufus about it. He was on duty that day and saw them."

"Fiona didn't say anything about what was wrong?" Joslyn asked.

Ruby shook her head. "But I didn't see her the last day she was here. I had taken a sick day."

"Is Rufus here today?"

"He's wandering around, just keeping an eye on things. Tall, lanky African-American man." Ruby reached out to grab Joslyn's hand. "Please find out what happened to Fiona. I hope it's nothing serious."

"We'll find her," Joslyn said. Fiona had left a hole in Joslyn's life when she left Los Angeles. Joslyn didn't have many women friends, and she always wondered if she might not have dated her abusive ex, Tomas, if Fiona had still been there with her frank opinions and logical insights. The least she could do was find out what happened to her friend now that it looked as if she'd gotten into something dangerous after she'd left the master's program in LA.

They had to circle almost the entire museum before they found Rufus, an older man so slender that his guard uniform hung loosely on him. He had a short, gray beard and almost completely bald head with his curly, gray hair cut short. As they approached him, he frowned at them as if he were trying to look menacing. "Something I can help you folks with?"

Then his eye fell on Clay, and his brows rose halfway up his forehead. "Well, I'll be. You look just like Fiona. You must be that brother she told me about."

Clay grinned and shook the man's hand. "Anything she told you about me, it wasn't true."

Rufus guffawed. "She said you'd say something like that." He nodded to Joslyn. "This your missus?"

Joslyn felt as if her head was in a furnace, and Clay turned redder than a beet. "I'm Joslyn. I'm an old college friend of Fiona's."

His handshake was firm, his fingertips calloused. "So you went to school with her in LA?"

"Yes, sir. She and I had most of the same classes."

"We're here looking for her," Clay said. "We hear she hasn't been around for a few weeks."

Rufus sighed heavily. "Don't know what's happened to her. I'm worried. It didn't seem like she was into anything shady, but that man she met with the last time she was here seemed awful slick, if you know what I mean."

"Who was he?" Joslyn asked.

"This older guy, although not quite as old as me. Seems like nobody's quite as old as me, these days." He flashed a grin, his smile bright in his dark face. "He was sitting and chatting with Fiona, and she looked pretty shaken."

"You didn't hear what they talked about?" Joslyn asked.

"Naw, I was standing by the door. There were some high school boys in the next room making fun of the abstract art, so I was keeping an eye on them in case they got rowdy."

"Maybe she and the guy were friends," Joslyn said.

"No, she didn't come in with him. She was alone when I saw her enter the front door—she gave me a smile and a wave—and this guy came and met her in the antique Chinese art room only half an hour later. She seemed surprised to see him, so I don't think she was intending to meet him here. They only talked five or ten minutes, but it was enough to make Fiona look upset and leave the museum early."

"Did he leave with her?"

"Nope. He sat in the Chinese room for another few minutes—looked sorta down, if you ask me—and then he left."

"Anyone with him?" Clay asked.

"Nope. But he was wearing some fancy suit, like those rich guys. I wouldn't be surprised if he had a driver waiting outside."

"I wonder why she was upset," Joslyn said. "Did Fiona say anything to you before she left?"

"No, she just smiled and waved, but she looked kinda distracted," Rufus said. "Sometimes she chats with me, sometimes not. But that was the last time I saw her. No police have been by, so I wondered if maybe she was on vacation or something. But I think she'd've told me if that was the case. It must have been that guy."

"You said he was slick."

"Dressed real smart, navy suit—even in this heat—and big silver cufflinks on his sleeves."

Clay had suddenly stilled. "What did he look like?"

"Oh, roundish face. Black hair, but receding like there was no tomorrow."

"Kind of heavy-lidded eyes?"

Rufus's eyebrows rose again. "Yeah."

If Clay knew who the man was, Joslyn would have expected him to be more triumphant. Instead, he seemed even more perplexed. "Do you know him?" she asked.

Clay was frowning at the floor. "I think so, but it doesn't make sense."

"Why not?"

He looked up at her, and his eyes had turned a stormy gray. "I think that was Martin Crowley—her father, and my stepfather."

THREE

Why would Fiona disappear after talking to Martin? As far as Clay knew, they were still on comfortable terms. Maybe not chummy, but not at odds with each other. And Martin wouldn't do anything to hurt Fiona, no matter what he'd done to Clay.

The memories, more bitter than medicine, burned his tongue and throat, and he swallowed to get them out of his system. Even after all these years, it still made him react as if his stepfather's utter rejection of him had happened yesterday.

"Her father?" Rufus said. Clay had forgotten he was still there. "Now that's interesting. Fiona never seemed happy when she talked about her daddy. And she certainly wasn't happy that man had come to talk to her that day."

Joslyn had been shocked when Clay had said the man was Martin, but now she looked thoughtful. "Can you remember anything else?" she asked Rufus.

He pursed his mouth, but then shook his head. "Sorry, I didn't hear anything that they said, and that's about all I saw."

Joslyn handed him her business card. "If you remember anything else, give us a call."

"Sure thing."

As they headed out of the museum, Clay said, "You didn't seem surprised that Fiona and Martin hadn't seemed very friendly that day. Fiona had always been pretty close to him."

Joslyn tilted her head. "Well, she was closer to Martin when I first knew her, but, especially just before she left Los Angeles, he seemed to annoy her or upset her more often. She never wanted to talk about him. I guess in the past two years, they never healed the breach."

"He must have said something to her to make her upset. But he can't possibly have anything to do with her disappearance. He wouldn't hurt her."

"But the fact is that sometime after he spoke to her, she went missing."

"If she were in danger from Martin, he'd have taken her at the museum, and he wouldn't have bothered to speak to her first." Clay sighed. "Plus I have a hard time believing Fiona would be involved in anything shady that Martin might be doing." He remembered his last big argument with Fiona in Chicago, and the reason she'd moved away from him.

"He might have helped her leave. If she was in trouble and he could help, she'd accept it."

He remembered Fiona's thready voice during their phone conversation. "The thing is, if she were safe with Martin, she wouldn't have asked us for help. My phone call and your postcard happened after she disappeared."

"Maybe it wasn't her?"

"It sure sounded like her. I knew her voice immediately."

Joslyn blew out a breath. "And the handwriting on that postcard was pretty close to hers. I recognized it."

Clay rubbed his forehead. He knew what he had to do, but didn't like being forced to approach Martin again, like a servant asking for a favor. "I have Martin's extension at his office. I'll give him a call and ask about Fiona."

The look Joslyn gave him implied that she understood what he hadn't said, saw the emotions churning in his gut whenever he thought of Martin. But she also understood, as much as he did, that Fiona came first.

There was a small hallway off the front foyer of the museum that offered them some privacy, so he headed there and pulled out his cell phone. He found Martin's phone number and dialed.

He tasted acid at the back of his throat as the phone rang. When a man's voice answered, he almost couldn't speak and had to swallow before he said, "Martin? This is Clay."

"I'm sorry, Mr. Crowley's not available at this time. This is his assistant. May I help you?"

Clay felt both relief and frustration. "Please ask him to call his stepson as soon as possible. It's about Fiona." He gave his phone number, but he had a feeling Martin wouldn't call him back. Not to be dramatic, but simply because to Martin, Clay didn't matter.

When he hung up, Joslyn asked, "He wasn't in?"

"I left a message, but Martin doesn't always return my calls." Actually, Martin almost never returned his calls.

"He might since this is about Fiona."

"But if he's involved in all this, he's not going to want to talk to us."

She sighed. "I'm afraid you're right."

They exited the front double doors of the museum into the bright sunlight, and the heat slapped him like a ten-foot wave. Clay had to pause to adjust to the change in temperature. That's when he saw it.

Just a slight movement from the farthest end of the parking lot stretched out in front of them. Clay squinted in that direction, but didn't see the movement again.

He'd lost the men following them, hadn't he?

"What is it?" Joslyn's voice was low but sharp. Her eyes also scanned the parking lot.

"I thought I saw...I don't know what I saw."

"How could they have found us?" Deep in thought, she began lightly rubbing a strange-shaped scar above her left eye. It seemed she wasn't aware she was doing it. "Maybe your rental car...I'll have to check it."

"Check what?"

"Maybe they put a tracker on your car or mine when we were at Fiona's office."

"That's kind of high-tech. Then again, if they're the same guys who rigged Fiona's house, I guess I believe they could do it." Clay kept sweeping his gaze over the parking lot even as they headed to his car.

"Don't unlock it just yet." Joslyn began circling the car, checking the rims, finally dropping onto the sizzling asphalt to check the underside of the vehicle. "I don't see anything."

Clay hadn't stopped looking around, but they were the only ones moving around out here. The other cars in the lot seemed empty, and he couldn't see the white Taurus, although many of the cars were white. He'd noticed that about Phoenix—lots of white and light-colored cars, probably to combat the heat. "Let's get out of here."

The inside of the car was a furnace and he cranked up the air-conditioning.

"Even if we don't know for sure that they

followed us here, we should take precautions," she said.

"Like what?"

"Maybe there's a tracker on our clothes. Or maybe they found a way to clone one of our cell phones, and that's how they're trailing us."

"People can do that?"

"It takes special equipment, but yeah."

And men who had access to explosives might have access to that kind of equipment. "Okay, so where to?" He backed out of the parking stall.

"The nearest mall."

Clay kept an eye out behind them as they drove, but he couldn't spot a tail if there was one. He had done his fair share of tailing people back in his mob henchman days, but even then, he hadn't been great at noticing them following him. How ironic that he could have used some of his criminal skills now. Still, he didn't regret getting out of that life, paying his dues. He just wished he could feel as though he had finally settled that debt.

There was a mall a few miles away that looked rather new, with a cluster of golden-red buildings rising up at the side of a freeway, surrounded by empty lots of stone and dirt. "Is this good?" he asked.

"Yes. We don't want anything too upscale. They may not have the burner phones we need."

They walked through the outdoor mall until

they found a phone kiosk, and Joslyn bought several burner cell phones.

"We need that many?" Clay asked.

"You never know." After Joslyn had paid using cash, they walked away and she said, "Plus, I noticed the kiosk didn't seem to keep good records. If anyone knows we went here, they might have a hard time figuring out which phones we bought, and their numbers."

"That's good thinking." He'd had to find people for his bosses every so often, but it had never been an intricate business like this, and he'd never had to try not to be found.

The next stop was clothes shopping, so they could replace the ones they were wearing, just in case they were being tracked that way. There wasn't an all-in-one clothing shop at this mall, so they went to a men's store first. "I can't just get athletic shorts and a T-shirt?" he asked her.

"If we need to talk to people, they'll respond better if you're better-clothed."

"I don't need a suit, do I?" Clay inwardly groaned. He wasn't uncomfortable wearing a suit, but in this heat, it would be torture, even though all of the places had air-conditioning.

Joslyn's eyes twinkled like chips of amber, as if she could guess what he was thinking. "No. Just something that doesn't look like you just played basketball with the fellas."

He found some khaki shorts and a short-sleeved

polo shirt, which he wore out of the store, and carried his old clothes in a bag. He caught Joslyn looking at him appreciatively as he stood in line to pay. When she saw he had noticed, she blushed and turned away.

Other women had given him double takes often enough for him not to be embarrassed by it, especially since he'd grown stronger and dropped some of his body fat through his training at his local mixed martial arts gym. But Joslyn's glances somehow made him stand a little taller.

They headed to a women's clothing store next. Clay scanned the faces in the crowd, and because of his height, he could see over most heads, but he didn't notice anyone who looked like the men in the white Taurus. It was hard to tell if anyone was following them in the crowd since most people were going from store to store, like they were, so he saw several people more than once.

Clay was used to women who browsed slowly along the clothing racks, but Joslyn surprised him by glancing quickly over the clothes and grabbing an outfit similar to what she was wearing—khaki pants and a navy blue polo shirt.

He didn't know why he did it, but his hand closed over hers as she lifted the hanger off the rack. "Wait. You're not getting that, are you?"

She frowned at him. "Of course I am."

"Look, I'm no fashion expert, but how about we get you something that matches what I've got?"

"It matches. Polo shirt, khakis."

"Not for a girl. It makes you look like a sales clerk."

"But it's what you're wearing."

He couldn't quite explain it, and he was muddling things up by trying, so he looked around, and then grabbed a sundress in light blue and brown. "How about this?"

She looked at him as if he'd grown two heads. "I don't...wear dresses."

He stared at her. "Ever?"

"Well, I've worn dresses, of course, but usually..." She looked flustered. "I don't know, it's just kind of...girly."

"But you're a girl."

"I know that." She glared at him.

He tried another tactic. "You said it yourself—if we talk to other people, they respond better if we're better clothed. It's less intimidating if we look like a couple. And we'd look more like a couple if you wear a dress rather than pants and a polo shirt."

She knit her brows as if she wasn't sure she quite believed him, but she took the dress and put it back. He was about to argue when she said, "It's the wrong size." She grabbed another one and headed to the changing rooms.

Clay blew out a breath. She was nothing like the other women he'd known. Joslyn seemed more masculine in some ways, carrying herself as if unaware of her body, and yet she was so beautiful.

She stepped out of the changing room, and despite the scowl on her face, the image of her in the sundress made his heart stop for a moment. Her collarbones rose above the modest neckline and her arms were bare, showing off her delicate bone structure. The skirt swirling above her knees floated around the curves of her figure.

"What is it?" She looked faintly alarmed.

"Nothing," he said quickly. "You're just...you look captivating." The word was more romantic than he'd intended, but it just popped out, and it described exactly what she was.

Joslyn turned a deep red and looked away. It seemed as if she were struggling with some memory. Then she took a deep breath and seemed to regain her composure. "Is this fine?" Her voice was businesslike.

He couldn't help it. He reached out to run the backs of his fingers down the side of her face.

She stilled, like a deer in the woods, her amber eyes wide. Her skin was soft, and the feel of it sent tingles up his hand, his forearm, his shoulder.

Then someone accidentally bumped into him from behind, and the moment was over.

"I'll go pay for this." She walked away before he could say anything.

Not that he could have said anything. That one

touch had shaken him, and he wasn't sure why or what to do about it.

Nothing. He was a man haunted by his past mistakes, and no woman would want to saddle herself with that.

They went to a shoe store to get new loafers for Clay and sandals for Joslyn, which were a far cry from the heavy Doc Martens she'd been wearing, but which matched the dress better and lengthened her legs even more. At the store, she was also able to get a new purse, as large as a tote bag.

"Do you really think we've got trackers on our clothes?" he asked as they walked back to the car.

"Better to be safe than sorry. We should probably throw them in the trash…" She stared at the parking stall. "Wasn't our car here?" Instead of his gold-colored Nissan rental, a silver pickup truck stood in its spot.

"Maybe we're on the wrong row." He strode down a different one, but he was almost certain it was wrong. He remembered that they'd gotten out of the car and the section had led directly to the children's clothing store at the edge of the mall.

They circled the lot, and Clay hit the button on the remote as he walked, but there was nothing. Finally they returned to the spot he'd thought he'd parked the rental.

There was no denying it. Someone had stolen his car.

* * *

"This is too coincidental." Joslyn could only stare at the pickup truck. It must have parked in their spot right after their car had been taken.

"But what would anyone have to gain by stealing a rental car?" A muscle twitched in Clay's jaw.

"I don't know."

Clay's hands opened and closed into fists as he paced in front of the truck. The action reminded her a little of Tomas when he became angry, and she couldn't stop the blip of panic at the sight.

God had protected her once, and she'd trusted that He'd protect her again, especially if she was careful about the situations she'd put herself into. But since coming to Phoenix and meeting Clay, the situation had gotten more and more unpredictable.

Yet a part of her seemed to sense that while Tomas had let his temper get out of control, Clay wouldn't cross that line.

Then again, she'd been wrong about Tomas. How could she know that she wouldn't be wrong about Clay?

"Let's get a cab to Fiona's workplace, since my car is there," she said.

Clay blew out a long breath and put his hands on his hips, then his back lost that stiffness and he turned to her with an expression still frustrated, but calmer. "You're right. I'll call them now. And I have to call the rental company, too."

Joslyn was surprised she hadn't had to do more than suggest it. Tomas would have said… But Clay wasn't Tomas, was he?

In that clothing store, the way he'd looked at her had made her feel…

She hadn't been attracted to a man in a long time. Her last relationship had been so disastrous that she had walled off her heart and her senses. But now it seemed she was changing, and she wasn't sure she wanted it that way. She still felt vulnerable after all she'd lost.

She closed her mind to that thought. She couldn't think about her losses, because then the pain would grip her again and it would take too much time and effort to make it let go.

Her eyes refocused on Clay, who was on the phone with a cab company. Fiona had spoken warmly, although a bit sadly, about her brother. She could see aspects of Fiona in Clay, their friendliness to others, their protectiveness. And like Fiona, Clay made Joslyn think differently about herself.

At the clothing store, he had made her feel feminine. She was used to being around men because of her major in software engineering, but even the women she met had been tomboyish like her.

But not Fiona. She'd tried to get Joslyn out of her shell, going out more, interacting with other people more.

Clay had pulled her even further out, shattering her habit of thinking of herself as "one of the guys." He'd had difficulty in explaining why, but he'd wanted her to wear that dress. And she didn't understand why she'd listened to him.

After all, Tomas had done the same thing—bought her dresses, told her she was beautiful. Since that episode in her life, she'd retreated to her old fashion sense, which consisted of pants and shirts, practical garments that were similar to what the other engineers wore. So why had she listened to Clay about the sundress? Wasn't this a bad thing?

Luckily she'd brought her side flashbang gun holster with her on this trip, so she hadn't had to worry about a visible gun harness for her firearm. She'd only recently gotten her Concealed Carry Permit, since she started working for the O'Neill Agency.

Clay hung up. "The cab should be here in a few minutes. And the rental company said they'd file the police report since they have GPS tracking on the car."

"Speaking of trackers, since we're dumping our clothes, maybe we should ditch our cell phones, too, in case they managed to put a tracker in them or clone them."

"No, wait," Clay said. "Let's keep our cell phones for a little while."

"We should at least dismantle them so they can't trace the GPS—"

"No, keep them on. I have an idea."

But before she could tell him, the cab arrived. It drove them to Fiona's company parking lot so she could pick up her car. When the cab had left, Joslyn asked, "What now?"

"Let's go to my hotel."

"But the men after us will know you'll go back there."

"It's what I'm hoping for," Clay said.

She looked at him strangely. "Does this have to do with the cell phones?"

"Yup. Let's go."

His hotel was close to Fiona's house, which was unfortunately halfway across town, so it took them the better part of an hour before they were finally pulling into the hotel parking lot. There were a couple police squad cars parked outside the front doors. Clay's shoulders were bunched as he saw them. Joslyn wondered if it was a throwback to his time working for that mob family. He certainly wouldn't have been happy to see the police back then.

However, as she drove past the squad cars, there was suddenly loud shouting. She instinctively hit the brakes.

Then they were surrounded by police officers. Joslyn glanced at Clay, but he had the same perplexed look. "What do we do?" she asked.

"Get out of the car, I guess."

She turned off the engine and slowly got out of

the car. Clay opened the passenger side door and cautiously stood up, his hands raised.

And instantly the officers were slamming him face-first against the side of the car and slapping handcuffs on him.

"What's going on?" Joslyn said. The officers weren't bothering with her.

"Clay Ashton, you're under arrest," one officer said.

"For what?" he demanded.

"A hit-and-run accident. You put a kid in the hospital."

FOUR

Joslyn reined in her temper as she exited the police station. It wasn't the fault of the officer behind the reception desk that they couldn't give out any information about Clay, but she still felt like kicking something.

The Arizona heat was a slap in the face after the slightly sour smell of the police station waiting room, where she'd spent the better part of the last hour. She needed to regroup and figure out her next move, but she wouldn't be able to do it there.

The worst part was not knowing what the right course of action was. Everything about this situation was out of her hands—she couldn't find out what charges Clay was being held on, she didn't know anything about the two men who were after them and worst of all, Fiona was missing and they had no idea where she was or if she was even alive.

She shivered despite the heat. She had to believe Fiona was still alive.

Right now, she had to find out how to exonerate Clay. She remembered what Fiona had said about her brother, and now that she'd met him, Joslyn found it easy to trust him. She'd had to relearn how to trust people after she'd escaped from Tomas. Something about Clay was so open, so earnest. He had that sadness behind his eyes every so often, but it never seemed he was trying to hide anything.

Her cell phone rang, and she didn't recognize the number, but she answered. "This is Joslyn."

"Oh, good, I did remember your phone number right." Clay breathed out a sigh of relief.

"Clay! Are you calling from the police station?"

"Yeah, my one call. I gotta make this quick. Know any good lawyers?"

She could call her boss Elisabeth, who probably knew some good lawyers. Elisabeth seemed to have a million contacts. "Did you do it?" Joslyn asked.

"Not unless I was in two places at once. It happened at noon today, with my rental car. They got an 'anonymous tip' about it. I tried to explain the car was stolen from the mall parking lot, but the detective didn't believe me." His voice ended on a bitter note.

"That's not enough to hold you."

"They can hold me for forty-eight hours without cause. I think they're suspicious because of my record and the explosion at Fiona's house."

"We were the *victims* there."

"You're preaching to the choir."

"Okay, I'll figure out something." She already had an idea, thanks to the training she'd gotten at the O'Neill Agency. "Sit tight, don't say anything."

"I know the drill." Clay paused, then said, "Be careful, okay? We know there're two guys after us, and if they're involved in this, then you're on your own. Watch your back. Stay in public places."

"I know the drill," Joslyn said soberly. As she hung up, she knew he was right. It wasn't good for her to be alone right now. She missed having him to guard her back.

She didn't want to rely on Clay—on anyone, really—but it was strange that she'd come to depend on him in only the few hours she'd known him. His quick reflexes and protective instinct had already saved her from that bomb, and his friendly nature had enabled them to get some information from Ruby and Rufus at the art museum. Elisabeth always told Joslyn that her questioning sounded more like a police interrogation.

Realizing how much she might need his help made her feel vulnerable. Which was silly. She was vulnerable to those two thugs who were after them, not to Clay.

Well, she was no longer that timid, shy girl dependent on a big, brawny boyfriend—Tomas had cured her of that. The O'Neill Agency had taught her lots of skills, including how to stay safe.

And how to prove her whereabouts. Or in this case, Clay's whereabouts at noon.

First, she gave her bosses a call, but got their voice mail. She left a message explaining the situation, and asked for a recommendation for a lawyer here in Arizona.

She got in her rental car and drove back to the mall. Retracing their steps, she checked the store fronts for cameras, but found none. So she went into the men's clothing store they'd entered first and asked to speak to the manager.

While she was waiting, she tried to relax her face and body. It wouldn't do her any good to look as tense and stressed as she felt.

The manager approached, a bored-looking man in his forties with dark hair and swarthy skin. His nameplate read Edgar.

"Mr. Edgar—"

"Just Edgar," he said. "How can I help you, miss?"

"I'm Joslyn Dimalanta, with the O'Neill Agency." She handed him her business card. "I'm hoping you can help me out."

He flicked a glance at her card, but said nothing.

"I came in here with my friend about two hours

ago. He bought some clothes. But the police are insisting he was across town in a hit-and-run accident at the exact same time."

"Look, I'm sorry for your friend, but what does that have to do with me?"

"Would you be able to call the police and show them your store video feed?" Joslyn pointed to the discreet camera, which covered the cashiers at the front of the store. "It can prove my friend was here and not at the accident scene."

Edgar sighed and rolled his eyes. "Sure, sure. I'll call them tonight after the store closes."

"You couldn't do it now? He's at the police station—"

"He's not going anywhere, and I'm busy right now." He nodded to the cashiers, who were all busy with customers. "It'll have to be later, okay?" He suddenly remembered he was talking to a customer and added, "I'm sorry. Is there anything else I can do for you?"

Hold still so I can bop you in the nose. She forced a smile. "No."

He walked away. He hadn't even asked the name of her friend in jail.

As she exited the store, her jaw hurting from her gritted teeth, Joslyn reflected that maybe the time stamp on the store wouldn't even be close to the time of the accident. After all, they'd hit this store first, after parking the car.

She went to the women's clothing store, but

the manager had stepped out for a few minutes, so Joslyn said she'd be back later. Then she made her way to the shoe store.

She asked to see the manager, and while she was waiting, she tried to figure out what she could say so that it wouldn't be a repeat of her experience with Edgar. *Lord, please just tell me what I should do to fix this.*

The manager was a woman with short, dark hair that framed her pixie face, but her walk was straight and confident. She held out her hand and gave a friendly smile. "Jody Mills. How can I help you?"

Joslyn squeezed her hand a little harder than necessary. "I'm sorry to bother you like this, but I need your help."

Jody's eyebrows rose. "My help?"

"I'm Joslyn Dimalanta, and I work for the O'Neill Agency." She handed Jody her business card. "I'm in the area with a friend, Clay Ashton, searching for his sister. We're very worried about her."

"You think she was here?" Jody looked around her store.

"No, but we were here earlier today because we needed a change of shoes." Joslyn shrugged. "It's a long story. Anyway, at the same time, our rental car was stolen and used in a hit-and-run, and Clay is in jail because the police think he did it." Joslyn nodded to the security cameras.

"Do you think I could look at your store video feed? It might show Clay and me here around the same time as the accident, which would prove he couldn't have been involved."

Jody's shoulders straightened. "Of course. That should be easy enough." She led the way to her office on the far corner of the store, a nondescript door with just a small sign that said Employees Only. They walked down a short, narrow hallway, passing a staff break room on the right, then to an unmarked door.

Inside, a man with a round face, gray-brown beard and merry eyes looked up from where he sat in front of several video monitors. "Yeah, boss?" He had a slight Southern accent.

"Hey, Benny," Jody said. "We need to see some video from earlier today, around…?" She looked at Joslyn.

"Around noon," Joslyn said.

"I'll pull up from eleven o'clock on." Benny fiddled with the security video computer, punching in commands at the keyboard, then nodded toward a monitor and chair at the desk behind him. "Coming up right over there."

"Thanks, Benny." Jody sat at the chair and Joslyn stood to one side.

The screen was split into the four video cameras in the store. Jody moved the mouse at the computer and the feed went into fast forward. Joslyn kept her eye on the video that showed the front door, and as soon as she saw herself and Clay enter, she said, "Stop, there we are."

Jody squinted at the video. "Yup, there you are."

They watched the videos as it showed them shopping for shoes and finally paying for them. The timestamp showed them entering the store at 11:37 and leaving at 11:55 pm.

Joslyn sighed and passed her hand over her eyes. Even if Edgar had let her see the video, it would have been the wrong timestamp to prove Clay hadn't been involved in the accident. *Thank You, Lord.*

"Your friend's being held by the police right now?" Jody asked.

Joslyn nodded. "Would you mind calling the police to come look at this? It'll prove Clay couldn't have been in the hit-and-run."

"No problem." Jody used the phone sitting on the desk next to the computer. "Mall security will call the police and escort them here."

"Thank you so much for doing this for me. I can't begin to tell you how much I appreciate it."

"You poor thing. You must be so stressed and worried."

"What's worse is that the more we're delayed, the further behind we are in our search for Clay's sister."

"When did she disappear?"

"About three weeks ago. Fiona Crowley?"

Jody shook her head. "Sorry, don't know her." She nodded to the frozen shot of Clay at the cash register and flashed Joslyn a grin. "He's a cutie, though. Just a client?"

Joslyn felt her face burst into flame. "Um… yeah."

Jody laughed. "What do you do for the O'Neill Agency?"

They chatted about Joslyn's work until a police officer, accompanied by a mall security guard, knocked on the door to the security room.

"Hey, Jody," said the mall security guard, "this is Officer Winchester. He's a buddy of mine."

"Nice to meet you." Officer Winchester had a deep voice and a self-assured air about him. He shook Jody's hand.

"Thanks for coming," Jody said. "This is Joslyn Dimalanta."

His large hand engulfed Joslyn's, and his grip was strong.

"So what's this about?" Officer Winchester asked.

"I have a friend in police custody right now," Joslyn said. "The detectives say that his rental car was involved in a hit-and-run accident at noon today, and they won't believe that he was here with me, because he spent some time in jail."

Officer Winchester's face was impassive.

Joslyn pointed to the video. "This is video feed from Jody's store that proves he was here at the same time as the accident. I'm hoping we can turn it over to you and you can give it to the detectives in charge of Clay's case."

Officer Winchester gave a firm nod. "I can do that. Could I see the video?"

They played it for him, fast-forwarding through the entire eighteen minutes that they were in the store.

"I'll take the video in," the officer said. "Jody, I'll need the originals."

"Could I get a copy first?" Joslyn asked. "Clay's lawyer is going to want to see it."

While waiting for Benny to make a copy for her, she said to Jody, "Thanks again. I don't know what I would have done if you hadn't been so helpful."

"Aw, sweetie, I could tell you were really worried. Of course I'd help. Besides, it was no skin off my back."

"Thank you for doing this for me. For Clay," Joslyn said to Officer Winchester.

His dark eyes were inscrutable, but he nodded. "I'll take this to the station, but I'm afraid I can't do anything else for your friend's case."

She knew he couldn't make her any promises, but she hoped he'd at least do what he said. She was waiting to hear from Liam O'Neill about that lawyer for Clay, and hopefully she could fix this entire frustrating situation.

As she was leaving the store she felt it. That

shiver across the back of her shoulders, that suspicion that she was being watched.

She had felt it often a few months ago, when she was on the run from Tomas, who had murdered her father. Most of the time, that feeling had been false, because if someone had been following her, Tomas would have found her a lot sooner than he had. She'd been paranoid and jumpy, exhausted by grief over her dead father and dead...

Her hand automatically went to her stomach and tightened there for a moment. Her counselor said she was making progress, but it still hurt like a physical pain.

Her shoulders tingled again. Was this the same thing, paranoia because of all the stress of the morning? It wasn't every day she was almost killed by a bomb. She knew she had compartmentalized it—her counselor would use the term *coping mechanism*—but she'd have to come to terms with it.

Later. Not right now.

"Hello, sweetheart." She didn't recognize the gravelly voice, but she recognized the man's face from the glimpses of him in the passenger seat of the car that had been following them this morning—his curly dark hair and sunglasses. He stood in front of her, blocking her way.

Stupid, stupid, stupid! If she'd been paying attention instead of taking a mental coffee break, she wouldn't have been surprised by him.

By *them*. The second man stood just behind his left shoulder.

Maybe she should have paid attention to the feeling she was being hunted.

She reacted quickly, instinctively. She shoved hard at the man and sent out a high-pitched scream. "Get away from me! Help! Officer Winchester!"

The policeman had been behind her when she left the store, but he'd turned left when she'd turned right. Was he still within hearing range?

People around them stopped to stare. When she shoved the man, he'd stumbled backward into a young man, who looked like a college student, leaning against the wall of a store. "Hey, man, watch it!" the student said.

The second man had sidestepped to avoid his partner's fall, and he moved in quickly to grab her elbow in a painful grip. "Let's go," he hissed.

She jabbed her fist into his throat.

He coughed, his grip loosened. She wrenched her arm away and ran back the way she'd come.

She wove through the crowd, her breath harsh in her ears. Was the man following her? Were they both following her?

Two firm hands grabbed her shoulders and stopped her. She was about to scream again when she looked up into Officer Winchester's stern face.

"Behind me," she said. "Two men."

He pushed her aside firmly to head back the way she'd come. She spotted a bench a few yards away and leaped onto it, scanning the crowd. She saw the two men running toward her, their expressions changing when they spotted Officer Winchester. They stopped, but the cop had seen them. They turned and bolted.

Soon the men's dark heads were at the edge of the crowd, then they tore away at a dead run to the parking lot. She tried to keep track of them, but they ducked behind a large minivan, and then she couldn't see where they went.

The policeman was too far behind, hampered by the crowds. When he finally got to the parking lot, he looked this way and that, but appeared to have lost track of them. The two suspects were smart and didn't go tearing out of the parking lot, drawing attention to their vehicle, and the lot was full enough that they could sneak around behind cars and avoid detection.

Joslyn hopped down from the bench and fought her way through the crowd to the parking lot. Officer Winchester was standing near an exit, scanning all the cars slowly leaving this section of the lot, but the men could also have driven out the other exit.

The policeman gave her a grim look. "Sorry, miss. Looks like we lost them."

FIVE

It was an unbearably sweet sight for Clay to see Joslyn outside the police station, holding out to him a paper bag with grease stains along one corner.

She smiled. "Fiona mentioned you liked bacon cheeseburgers. Is that still the case?"

"You are a dream come true."

She laughed, then turned to his lawyer. "I bought one for you, too, Ms. Harnett."

"Call me Jo." The blonde lawyer smiled broadly. "And I *love* bacon cheeseburgers."

Elisabeth Aday had come through for Joslyn and Clay. Since Elisabeth still volunteered at a local domestic abuse shelter, she knew several lawyers, and one of them had put in an urgent call to his friend Joanna Harnett in Phoenix. Joslyn had given Jo the copy of the video. Officer Winchester had apparently delivered the original video to the detective in charge of Clay's case as promised, but the lawman had been stubborn about releasing Clay even when faced with clear evidence that he was innocent. Jo had pulled strings, because Clay was finally released an hour later.

They sat on a bench outside the police station to eat their burgers. The salty bacon, melting cheese and juicy beef was exactly what he needed after the frustrating afternoon in police lockup.

None of the people he talked to would believe him. He'd spent two years in jail for being a low-level thug for that Chicago mob family, and he'd gotten a good job as a bouncer for a nightclub in the years since he'd been out, but none of that mattered to them. He felt as if he would never be able to escape his past.

All he wanted to do was to find Fiona, to apologize to her for that last fight they'd had before she left Chicago. To show her that he'd changed. To make up for all the grief he'd put her through.

"The detective will look into the accident," Jo said around a mouthful of burger. "It wasn't on a street with many businesses, so there isn't a good chance some bank ATM camera caught it on film or anything like that." She had a slight Southern lilt to her voice.

"I don't understand why they'd do that," Clay said. "They tried to kill us with that bomb at Fiona's house, then they followed us, but then they arranged to have me arrested. That's like a step back."

"We still don't know for sure that they're the ones who set the bomb," Joslyn said. "But...I think I know why they wanted you arrested—to take you out of the picture. To separate us."

Clay's shoulders grew rock hard. "What happened?"

"They tried to kidnap me at the mall." She spoke quickly, as if nervous about telling him.

"What?!" And he'd been stuck in a cage, unable to protect her. What good was he if he couldn't protect people?

"It was fine, a police officer happened to be right there," she said. "But they ran and he couldn't catch them. It was the same officer who delivered the security video of you in the shoe store to authorities."

"That was smart of them," Jo said reluctantly. "Separate the two of you so they could more easily grab Joslyn. Then with Clay in jail, they could afford to wait and take care of him later."

Joslyn swallowed. "That's what I was thinking. They're probably upset you got Clay out of jail so fast."

"They could've tried something," Clay said, "but I wouldn't go down so easily."

"What are you going to do now?" Jo wiped her mouth. She'd inhaled that burger.

"We still don't know where Fiona is or why she disappeared," Clay said.

"I want to get online to do some research on

Fiona and Martin Crowley," Joslyn said, "but I can't do that if we're being followed. Those men would interrupt us before I even had a chance to log in to my computer."

"Those creeps have to know something about Fiona. I want to set a little trap so we can find out more about them."

"Nope, I don't want to hear this." Jo stood. "As your lawyer, I don't want to know."

"We won't do anything illegal," Clay said. He'd learned his lesson years ago and was still paying for it now.

"Regardless, it's probably best if you don't tell me." Jo smiled at the two of them. "I hope I'll see you again, but maybe somewhere other than the police station."

"You bet." Clay shook her hand. "Thanks a lot."

Joslyn watched the lawyer walk away. "She was nice."

"And effective. The police could have been stubborn and kept me locked up."

"Not all policemen are like that."

"It's because of what I used to do. I've never had a good relationship with cops." And it looked as if he never would.

Joslyn leaned forward on the bench. "So what kind of trap did you want to set?"

"Where's your cell phone?"

"I left it on, like you wanted me to, but at the hotel so they wouldn't know where I was going."

She blew out a breath. "It didn't matter because they probably just followed me from the police station."

"But since it's still on, those guys may not realize we suspect the phones are trackable." Clay held up his own phone, which the officers had returned to him. "I want to lure them in. We'll drop the cell phones somewhere, make them think we're there, while we hide nearby. We can find out their license-plate number, maybe snap some photos."

Joslyn narrowed her eyes at him. "Tell me you're not also hoping to capture one of them."

Clay thought he'd be able to take them, although it would be a tough fight, but there was always the chance one of them would grab Joslyn. He didn't want to put her in danger or allow the men to use her as leverage. But he hesitated a fraction of a second too long before saying, "No."

"Clay—"

"Really, no. It's too dangerous. But it might be dangerous to set this trap for them, even if all we're doing is getting a look at them."

"Get me a good photo," Joslyn said. "I have a facial-recognition program I'm working on that can scan the web to try to find them."

"Really? I thought that was only on TV."

"You'd be surprised what real-life hackers can do."

He nodded and stood. "You ready?"

They tossed their trash and then got into Joslyn's rental car, although Clay got behind the wheel. "Let's get your phone and then make sure we're not being tailed," he said. "We need to be a few minutes ahead of them."

They went to Joslyn's hotel where they picked up her cell phone, and she gathered her things and checked out of the room, just in case. She seemed to have very few things—she'd bought new clothes at the mall today, and only had one other change of clothing. As she was looking through her stuff, she suddenly held up a small electronic device.

"Is that a...?" Clay said.

"GPS tracker." Her skin flushed. "They went into my hotel room and pinned it under the collar of my jacket."

"Don't ditch it yet," Clay said. "That way the men won't know that we discovered the trackers just yet. We can get rid of all that stuff later."

Then he spent some time driving in circles and scouting out some of the parking lots in the Phoenix area. He looked at an empty business park parking lot, but decided against it. Once their pursuers saw it, they'd know something was up because there was no reason for Clay and Joslyn to be there. If the men suspected a trap, they wouldn't fall into it.

Then he saw a rather run-down Mexican restaurant with faded yellow walls and a dark brown roof. The parking lot at Casa Rafael was only partially filled, maybe because it was still early for dinner, but it was the type of cars and the men Clay saw near the building's front doors that decided it for him. He passed the restaurant parking lot, but turned in to the lot next to it, which was attached to a paint supply store. He parked in the farthest corner of the lot.

"Why here?" Joslyn asked.

"We don't want them to see our car and know we're near. Come on." He grabbed his cell phone. He had to plant it quickly before their pursuers got within sight of the restaurant.

They climbed over the low brick wall separating the two parking areas and walked halfway down the lot, where Clay dropped his phone on the ground. He was about to walk away when Joslyn said, "Wait."

She pulled out one of the burner cell phones she'd bought. She dialed, then answered on her cell phone and kept the call open. She put her phone on speaker, then dimmed the screen so it wouldn't be easily seen in the darkening twilight and slid it under a car parked near where Clay had dropped his cell phone. She held up the burner phone. "We can listen in when the men get near enough."

"That's brilliant." He grinned.

They scurried to hide behind some cars against the back wall of the parking lot where they wouldn't be seen. Clay made sure he could see the restaurant's front door, so he could see who was coming and going. Their hiding spot smelled like mold, and faintly of urine, but it was also shadowed. Unless someone was specifically looking to find them, they wouldn't be noticed.

"What made you choose this parking lot?" Joslyn whispered.

"I didn't want anyone getting hurt by those guys. They won't try anything dangerous here." He gestured with his head toward the restaurant. "Those big guys over there? Mexican gang members. Our friends will think twice before they cause a scene." At least, he was reasonably sure about that. He'd worked with enough criminals to know that the two men would spot the gang members immediately.

They didn't have long to wait. A white Taurus slid slowly into the parking lot. Unfortunately, they parked on the opposite side from where Clay and Joslyn were hiding.

Clay angled himself but couldn't get a good view of their car, so he darted behind the next car parked along the wall. He saw the two men walking toward the restaurant. They eyed the Mexican gang members loitering outside warily, and received sharp looks in return, but were allowed to enter the restaurant.

Here was his chance. Clay made his way across the parking lot, darting between cars on a convoluted path so he could keep out of sight of the gang members near the restaurant, until he could get a clear shot of the men's car. Luckily, it stuck out since it was parked near a black SUV and a souped-up pickup truck. He memorized the license-plate number, then made his way back to where Joslyn was hiding. He was halfway there when one of the gang members spoke.

"Eh, Manny, *cigarrillo?*" His voice carried clearly across the parking lot.

Clay froze automatically, his heart racing. He didn't speak Spanish and wasn't certain what the gang member had said. Then he replayed the words in his head. It sounded as if maybe the guy was only asking for a cigarette, not something like, "Hey, did you see that gringo sneaking across the parking lot?"

He ducked behind the car where Joslyn was crouched. "Here's the license-plate number." He rattled it off to her, and she nodded and repeated it as she memorized it.

Only a few minutes passed before the two men walked out of the restaurant again, their expressions dark. One of them pulled out his cell phone and began walking around the parking lot, holding it out and looking at it.

"He's finding the signal from our cell phones," Joslyn whispered.

The other man, however, rather than walking

with him, went around to the other side of the parking lot.

"What's he doing?" Joslyn whispered.

"Looks like he's searching for our car." Clay began to regret he hadn't parked farther away than the next parking lot. If they found Joslyn's rental car, they'd know Clay and Joslyn were nearby.

Joslyn quietly crept to the edge of the car, then darted behind the next one. She held out her burner phone, which had a camera, and began snapping pictures of the man as he walked near them.

He was shorter of the two, with curly, dark hair and a scruffy face. His button-down shirt stretched over a slight paunch, and Clay could see that his dark jacket was a bit large for him. He frowned fiercely at his phone as he walked, and didn't even glance in their direction.

Joslyn sneaked back to where Clay still crouched, and nodded. "Got the photos of this guy, but the other...?"

Then the curly-haired man's voice shot from her phone speaker, and Joslyn hurried to turn down the speakerphone volume. "They're not here. They figured out we cloned their phones and dumped them." He was near the car under which Joslyn's cell phone had been left on and holding the call. "Yeah, here's one. The other phone's around here somewhere."

The other man called across the parking lot, "Met, what car did she drive again?"

"Silver Taurus," Met answered. He picked up Clay's phone, then swore and threw it into some nearby bushes. "You're not going to find it."

"Let's just get out of here, then." The other man started toward where they had parked their car.

They needed the other guy's photo, and this was as good a chance as they might ever get. Clay glanced at the restaurant and saw that the men who'd been loitering outside had gone in. He grabbed Joslyn's phone and sneaked out from behind the car. He followed Met as he headed to the men's white Taurus, keeping low behind the cars, trying to get a better angle of the other man.

Clay ducked behind an SUV just as Met said, "Did you see that?"

"See what?" the other man said.

Clay's throat was tight, his heartbeat pounding in his ears as he stood perfectly still. There was a minute or two of silence, then the sound of shoes scuffing asphalt.

"Nothing," Met muttered. "Just get in the car, G."

Clay peeked out from behind the SUV. He wasn't at a great angle, but he could take a few pictures of the other man, whom Met had called G. He had straight, brown hair cut short over his high forehead, intent eyes and a square jaw. Clay found himself sizing the man up like he would an opponent in a sparring match at his mixed martial arts gym back home in Illinois. The man would have a reach advantage with his long arms, and he walked with athletic confidence. But Clay would be able to use his larger-boned frame to his advantage if he took him to the mat in a wrestling or jujitsu move.

Clay had only taken a few photos of G when Met suddenly turned in his direction. "He's over there, G!"

G pulled out a gun and fired at Clay.

Joslyn couldn't see Clay, but she heard the gunshot. She jumped, every nerve in her body firing. Was Clay all right? She had to help him.

There was a second shot, and she instinctively flinched. *Get yourself together, Joslyn.* She forced her frozen muscles to move and began making her way toward where she'd seen Clay go.

"No! You idiot!" Met said.

But it was too late. The sound of the gunshots drew gang members from inside the restaurant. They ran into the parking lot, some of them with guns in their own hands. They shouted, pointing to where Met and G stood, and started firing at them.

Joslyn used the confusion to duck behind a black Cadillac. She had a view of Met and G, although she still couldn't see Clay. She reached and took out her gun from the flashbang side hol-

ster in her bra. It wasn't very large caliber, owing
to its small size, but if she got close enough, she
could take a shot.

She gulped. That was assuming she'd be able
to pull that trigger against a human being and not
a paper target.

"Get to the car!" Met ducked behind an SUV.

"It's too far away!" G turned to the car next
to him and smashed the window. Wails from the
alarm rang out. Within seconds, the two of them
had scrambled inside and disabled the alarm, and
the engine roared to life.

She darted forward, then saw movement behind a car ahead of her. She froze.

Clay appeared behind the tailpipe of a Mustang. The sight of him made an ache pulse tightly
in her chest. He was okay.

He hadn't seen her yet, but he started toward
her.

No, they had to get to the car. She scuttled
around a motorcycle to kneel behind an SUV, and
Clay finally saw her. She waved her arm toward
the other parking lot.

He nodded and changed directions, heading
toward her rental car.

Gang members ran toward the two men in the
stolen car, their guns blazing, but G backed out
sharply, making the men scatter. He put the car
in gear and skidded out of the parking lot, bullets
pinging off the back of the car.

The two men had gotten away—in a different car. The license-plate number they'd gotten was all for nothing. He could only hope Joslyn's face recognition program would come through.

SIX

Joslyn ran as fast as she could after Clay without being seen by the gang members. Clay met up with her and pulled her behind a minivan. They crouched in its shadow, both of them breathing heavily.

She heard the gang members shouting to each other in Spanish. She hadn't taken Spanish classes since her undergrad years, but she thought she understood enough to realize that the men were confused rather than angry. From the sound of their voices, they were looking around the area where the car had been stolen. Good thing Clay had gotten away from that section of the parking lot during the chaos following the gunfire.

A gang member accidentally set off another car alarm, and his friends began yelling at him. Then the voices sounded fainter as the men moved away. Clay risked looking around the minivan to see about a dozen men walking toward the restaurant.

"They're moving away."

Joslyn rose as if to go, but Clay grabbed her hand and tugged her back down to sit on the asphalt. "Wait a minute or two, just in case."

She nodded. The light was starting to dim as the sun grew lower, so Clay's hair shadowed his face. The unbearable heat of day was still radiating from the ground, but she shivered in the aftermath of the gunfight.

He still had her wrist and must have felt her trembling. He took her hand and rubbed it between his own. Only then did she realize her fingers were shaking.

"You can reholster your gun," he said.

"I almost fired at the two men." Joslyn bit her lip. "I'm so thankful to God that I didn't have to."

The words came out in a rush, but Clay suddenly looked slightly uncomfortable. She'd been a Christian for less than a year, but she'd already gotten used to thinking of God beside her, never leaving her alone.

After an awkward heartbeat of silence, Clay said, "If you'd fired, the gang members might have known you were there."

"But the gang members were firing their guns."

"They'd recognize if the gunshot sounded different," Clay said. "I did, sometimes." Then his eyes slid away, and she knew he was thinking about his other life, working for that mob family.

She wanted to tell him that she wasn't any

different, that she'd done things she regretted, but she'd gotten a second chance. She hesitated, because she didn't know him very well and bringing up her past was still like a knife in her heart, so the words stuck in her throat.

She became aware of the silence of the early evening, aside from the rumble of traffic and the faint call of a distant police siren. "Let's go."

They made their way to the low wall that separated the two parking lots, got into Joslyn's rental car, and slowly drove away.

Clay let out a long breath. Then he slammed the palm of his hand against the steering wheel in frustration.

She jumped, and she had a flash of Tomas in his car, doing the same thing only minutes before using those hands to beat her. She flinched and closed her eyes for a moment. *Breathe. Tomas is in prison. You're safe now.*

When she opened her eyes, she was surprised by the regret on Clay's face. "I'm sorry, I didn't mean to startle you."

But there was that hint of confusion in his eyes, too. She knew her reaction had been a bit extreme, but she didn't want to explain. He looked as if he might have already guessed that someone had hurt her at some point. "What are you upset about?" She made her voice light, neutral.

"It was all for nothing."

"You didn't get a picture of the other guy?"

"Oh, I did." He dug in his pocket and passed her the phone. "But when they stole the other car, I didn't get the license-plate number."

"It's a longshot, but we can still track their white Taurus in case it was rented with a credit card. I'd need to get online." She suddenly gasped. "Stupid, stupid! Pull over the car, quick."

He looked over his shoulder, then signaled and pulled into a grocery-store parking lot without even questioning her. He was so trusting. He reminded Joslyn of her father... She closed off the thought.

Once they were parked he asked, "What is it?"

She was already halfway out of the car and opened the back door. She reached under the floor mat of the seat behind her and slid out her laptop. "I should have realized, but with everything that's been happening, I didn't even think about my computer." She set it on the trunk of the car and fired it up.

Clay had gotten out of the car to stand beside her. "Has that been in the car the whole time?"

"I didn't want to leave it in the hotel room, and I thought it would be safe in the car. But I've left my car unattended a few times." Why was it taking so long for her computer to turn on? Or was she just being impatient and paranoid?

"You think they got to your computer, too?" Clay said.

"Those guys cloned our cell phones. That takes

special equipment. We already know they're high-tech and financed. It would be nothing for them to break into a rental car, even with the car alarm." Something was definitely wrong with her computer. She closed the top and flipped it over, peering at the casing. Were those tool marks?

"Can they hack into your computer? Or would they just install a GPS tracker?"

"I'd like to think they couldn't hack into the computer. I don't think they'd have enough time. But a GPS tracker…" She rummaged in her bag and came out with the portable toolkit she carried with her. She used a screwdriver to unscrew the casing of her computer and peered inside.

She just wasn't as familiar with hardware as she was with software. Everything looked fine, there was nothing obvious like the tracker she'd found under her jacket collar, but still, she sensed it had been tampered with. She shook her head. Her boss was going to kill her. Well, Liam would rant a bit, but then Elisabeth would point out that Joslyn had done the right thing, to be safe rather than sorry. That decided things for her.

"Would you do me a favor and buy lighter fluid for me?" She gestured with her head toward the grocery store behind them. "Oh, and matches."

"Sure." Clay trotted off.

Joslyn removed her hard drive, then removed the platter, and by the time she was done, Clay had returned. "Let's go somewhere I can torch this and also where we can get rid of the clothes they tagged," she said. "We need somewhere remote so it'll be easier to destroy the hard drive without anyone seeing the fire." They hadn't ditched the clothes at the mall with the car being stolen, and Clay had wanted to take advantage of any trackers to try to trap them in that restaurant parking lot, but they needed to get rid of it all now.

Clay took the freeway out of downtown Phoenix and headed west, past Surprise and into the boonies. The sun was setting but the land was so flat that there was enough light to see how the roads formed a grid around squares of farmland or empty lots, waiting for development. Soon they found a piece of empty land several blocks away from the nearest housing development.

Clay parked along the side of the road on pitted dirt that made the car bounce and sway. They got out and headed toward the middle of the lot, which was hard rock, gravel and clay, scattered with stones and pieces of broken concrete.

Dropping her computer, the removed hard drive and the platter onto the ground, Joslyn squirted the hard drive and platter with lighter fluid. She didn't want to make the fire too high because then it would be too noticeable, but it had to be hot enough to melt the platter. Clay lit a match and tossed it on the pile.

"Let's get rid of our stuff, too," he said. "Anything they might have tampered with."

Nausea quivered in her stomach at the thought of those two men touching her things. She hadn't brought anything important with her on this trip to Phoenix. However, she'd only just started putting her life back together after Tomas was arrested last year, and she'd had to start from scratch. Getting rid of her things made her feel as if she was losing herself again, and she didn't like that lack of control over her life.

Get over it, you're just dumping some clothes. She went to get her bag from the car and made sure she wasn't leaving anything important that she might need. They dumped their bags next to the burning hard drive for the two men to find, if they bothered to come looking. She made sure the GPS tracker from her jacket was there.

"We should get a new car," Clay said as they started walking back to the car.

"I don't have the funds to buy a used car. Do you?"

He winced. "No. Another rental?"

"They all have LoJack."

"You think these guys have some kind of device where they can track our car's LoJack?"

"Probably not, but if they have the resources we think they do, they could hire someone to hack into the LoJack database."

"Then we should get rid of this car, stat."

"They won't be after us right away," Joslyn said. "It would take a hacker a bit of time to do it."

"I'd suggest public transportation, but those guys aren't squeamish about firing a gun in public places."

"They might be able to tap into traffic cameras anyway." She thought hard as they walked. "I need to get online—no, more than that. I need to run my facial-recognition program on those photos we got. That limits our options down to one." She stopped walking and faced him. "I need to go back to Sonoma."

His brows lowered over his eyes. "But Fiona…"

"The online research I need to do will help us find her, but I can't do it here. I need a more powerful computer than anything at an internet cafe, and I need a secure line. Besides, we don't know that she's still in Arizona."

He nodded slowly. "I see your point. So do we head to the airport?"

"Yes," she said, "but I don't think we should fly back. They got you arrested once already, so who's to say they won't do something like that again once we're inside the airport? Airport security takes any threat they hear about seriously."

"Driving will take longer."

"But there's fewer people around." And she'd feel more in control of the situation if it was just her, Clay, and the highway.

"So are we going to drive back with this rental?" They'd gotten to the car by now.

"No, I want to make it harder for them to track us. We'll get another rental."

"They won't be able to trace that, too?"

"Eventually they will, but to find it, they'll first have to figure out the credit card I'm going to use is connected to the O'Neill Agency."

They drove her car back to the company she'd rented it from and returned it, but then instead of heading to the main terminal, they walked outside and headed down the street. The car rentals were all clustered together in an industrial area, with the freeway, loud and breezy, only a block away.

The rental car agency she chose had a few people inside the glass reception room, but Clay grabbed her and pulled her to the side. "Let's wait awhile and go in when there isn't a crowd around to remember seeing us."

The sun had set and it was full dark by now, so there wouldn't be as many people coming in and out of the rental agency. "Okay," she said. They stood around the corner of the building, next to some planters full of flowers.

"What kind of research can you do on Fiona that you didn't do before?" Clay asked.

"I didn't know the connection with Martin. I want to know what Fiona might be running from—what she might have been involved in—so that we can know where she'd go."

"The opposite of what she's running from."

"Yes."

"Maybe Martin's enemies are after her," he said.

"Was Martin involved in anything shady?"

Clay gave a short bark of laughter. "I'm pretty sure he was, just from the little I knew about him."

She'd need to do some digging on the internet. "I was wondering if Martin talked to her to warn her, and that's why she ran."

"So Martin was helping her?"

"Wouldn't you want help against men who rigged your house to explode?"

"Yeah, true," he said. "It's just that I *know* Fiona wouldn't get involved in something that would get her in trouble."

He was so emphatic. Joslyn said hesitantly, "I don't think Fiona would do anything like that, but…it's hard to really know a person." Look at how much she thought she knew Tomas. "And you haven't seen Fiona in years."

He bent his head, his hair falling into his eyes. All she could see was the outside floodlight glinting in his gold-brown hair. "I know she wouldn't get into any kind of shady business because… well, that's the reason she left Chicago. Because of me and my shady business."

"The mob family? Fiona told me about that."

"She didn't want me involved with them. We had huge fights about it. Finally she threatened to leave the house we were sharing together." Clay sighed, raising his eyes to the night sky above. "I was young and stupid. The money was great and it beat having a desk job somewhere. I liked the excitement and the danger, plus I was good at it. And I didn't think she'd really leave."

"But she did."

"She didn't just move out of our house, she left Chicago. I didn't know where she went—I tried contacting Martin, but he wouldn't even return my calls."

"What?" The word flew out of her mouth before she could stop and think.

He gave her a strange look.

She felt heat rising from her jawline. "It's just…Martin knew Fiona was in Los Angeles. She mentioned to me about meeting with him regularly, since his main office building is there. Why wouldn't he return your calls just to tell you Fiona was safe?"

Clay looked away, and she could see the muscle leaping in his jaw. "We didn't have that kind of relationship," he said in a tight voice.

She knew they weren't close, but that kind of behavior was almost cruel. What kind of man was Martin Crowley?

She took a deep breath. "You said yourself, Martin loves Fiona. Why would he get her involved in anything illegal that he's doing?"

Clay frowned and stared at the ground as he thought about it.

"I don't know your history with Martin," she said. "You probably have a good reason for hating him. But anything that can help us find Fiona is important. Whatever feelings you have about Martin—try to set them aside for now. Don't let them cloud your judgment."

He frowned at her, and she wondered if she'd gone too far. But she continued, "We have to focus on finding Fiona."

At that, the thundercloud in his expression slowly blew away. "You're right."

"I don't think she's running from Martin. He cares about her. But he may hold the key to finding her. Since we got rid of our phones…"

"I'll call him again." Clay started dialing. He left a message on his stepfather's voice mail and then hung up, shaking his head.

"You can't say you didn't try," Joslyn said.

He nodded. She could clearly see the pain behind his eyes, and so she reached out to touch the back of his hand.

He flipped his hand over and clasped hers, squeezing once before letting go. He cleared his throat. "It's late, anyway. I didn't expect him to be at his office."

She noticed the people she'd seen inside the car rental office leaving. "I think we're clear."

"Wait." He reached out to one of the planters

and picked a blue flower, a bachelor's button. He handed it to her.

"Don't pick their flowers." But she was smiling.

"This is for you. Thanks."

She didn't say anything. She thought she knew why he was thanking her.

"I think I've been feeling this bitterness for so long, I've forgotten how to let stuff go," he said slowly.

She understood him. Grief was something she was learning to let go of, but it still seemed to consume her some days.

He then took the flower from her fingers and tucked it into her hair above her ear. "There. Perfect."

But his hand didn't move away from her face. The pads of his fingertips followed the curve of her cheek, softer than the touch of a feather. She looked up and was captured by his eyes, blue-gray and intent upon hers. She could smell cedar and oranges, all underlaid by the scent of his musk, that essence that was Clay.

There was a fluttering just under her ribcage, and she found it hard to breathe.

Then something in his eyes flickered, and he looked away. It was almost like…shame. His hand dropped.

"Let's get inside."

She closed her eyes, briefly, remembering the touch of his hand. She had to force herself to remember why Clay was all wrong for her, to remember that Clay reminded her too much of Tomas. And look how well that had turned out.

She shook her head to clear it, then followed him into the rental agency. Fiona was important now. And after they found her, it would be best if she never saw Clay Ashton again.

He'd wanted to kiss her.

Clay drove along the almost empty highway, an eye behind him for any headlights. He was tired, but his body was tense and on high alert. Joslyn had said it would take time before the two men they now knew as Met and G could figure out they'd rented this new car and headed toward Sonoma, but he wasn't taking any chances.

In the midst of all this danger, he'd wanted to kiss her. He'd known her for fewer than twenty-four hours, but with everything that had been thrown their way, he'd become more and more impressed by her. She was smart. What was more, she was logical. She was the complete opposite of everything he was.

He'd still wanted to kiss her.

She was beautiful, and capable, and confident, and yet there were signs that someone in her past had hurt her. He recognized that look because he'd met other women in situations like that. As a bouncer at a night club, he was friends with the waitresses and bartenders, many of whom were women, and once in a while, one of them would come in with bruises barely hidden by makeup. He'd sometimes walk them to their car or drive them home, but at the end of the day, he always felt helpless.

The thought made his hands clench around the steering wheel, but then he realized that might alarm Joslyn and he relaxed his grip.

He looked over at her. She was finally asleep, her head leaning against the window. She looked soft and vulnerable, not like the woman who'd pulled a gun, ready to fire at the two thugs after them and all the Mexican gang members in that parking lot. She'd been scared, but she'd been ready to do what she had to in order to protect them.

If he'd had a normal life and a normal past, he wouldn't mind getting to know her, all the facets of her personality, from her vulnerable side, to the woman with a Concealed Carry Permit, to the woman who had been hurt in her past.

But he didn't have a normal life—he'd worked for a mob family. He'd done terrible things that he couldn't undo. He'd gone to prison. He'd even chased away the only person who loved him, his half sister. He wasn't someone Joslyn ought to know.

Which was why he hadn't kissed her, even though everything inside of him wanted to. He protected people—sometimes the wrong people, like the criminals he'd worked for—but it was what he was best at. And so he knew that in order to protect Joslyn, he had to stay far away from her. There were too many things in his past that would horrify her.

She slept until he stopped for gas at a small town in central California. They'd made good time through LA because of the late hour, although there had still been traffic on the freeways, even after midnight. However, he'd been careful to avoid the larger gas stations in case it made it easier for the men to track them, and had picked this small mom-and-pop where he would pay with cash.

She stretched as he got back into the car. "What time is it?" She didn't wait for an answer and looked at her own cell phone, then yelped. "You've been driving the entire time?"

"It's okay, I couldn't have slept anyway."

"I'll drive from here on out," she said, unstrapping her seatbelt.

"I'm fine."

"Even if you were, I know how to avoid the traffic cameras in the Bay Area and in Sonoma."

She had a point. He unbuckled his belt and hauled himself out of the driver's seat. Once he'd sat in the passenger side—sliding the seat back to accommodate his longer legs—she had already adjusted her seat and the rear and side mirrors.

"Do you really think those guys could tap into the traffic cameras?"

"I'm not sure." She started up the car. "Their tech was pretty impressive, but traffic cams require a different type of hacking. Or illegal access."

"I think it's safe to assume they're financed pretty deeply. And wouldn't blink an eye at finding illegal access."

She said something in reply, but he didn't hear it because he was fast asleep.

When he woke, the sun was up and the briny scent of the ocean drifted into the car from her open window. They were on a freeway arching above city streets, and in the distance he saw the big cranes used to unload the containers from large ships.

"Clay."

He realized she'd called his name a few times. He was instantly awake. "What is it?"

"I think we're being followed."

SEVEN

In a flash, Clay had loosened the slack on his seat belt and twisted around to look out the back window. "Which car?"

"I think it's the white van. It's been behind me since San Jose."

"Where are we?"

"Oakland."

He wasn't familiar enough with California geography to know exactly where they were, but the ocean made him think they must be around San Francisco. "How far away from Sonoma?"

"About an hour."

There were a fair number of cars around them for midmorning, although it wasn't stop-and-go traffic.

"How'd they find us? Did they hack into the LoJack on our rental?" he asked.

"If that's the case, we would only be able to lose them temporarily, like in Phoenix. They'd find us again pretty quick."

The only way they'd lose their tail was to ditch the car. Which meant a cab or public transportation. Wait a minute…"Oakland, you said?"

She nodded.

"Head to the Oakland Coliseum."

She gave him a bewildered look.

"It's a major sports arena, so I'm betting there's some type of public transportation station nearby. We can park the car and catch a bus or a train."

"Oh! You're right. There's a BART station near the coliseum." She signaled right to change lanes.

"Don't signal," he said. "Just go."

"Oh, right." She took a sharp breath, then cut left, in front of a speeding Jaguar.

A horn blared, but she ignored it and sped up to pass the car that had been ahead of her. She cut right in front of a Buick and then right again. She exited the freeway with only a few yards to spare before the exit lane diverged.

Clay had held tight while she drove, but he'd gotten used to reckless driving in Chicago, before he'd gone to prison. However, he saw that Joslyn was white-knuckled as she gripped the steering wheel.

"They didn't follow us," he told her, lowering his voice so it would be more soothing. "It's okay."

She nodded but didn't speak.

"Pull into that McDonald's," he said. "We'll switch."

"Please."

She parked, and Clay jumped out and swung around to the driver's side. He opened the door for her and saw that her hands were shaking as she got out of the car.

He grabbed her hand. "You did great."

She closed her eyes briefly. "I hate driving."

"Then it's a good thing I like it." He squeezed her hand and felt her squeeze back.

He followed her instructions to get them to the Oakland Coliseum, praying there wasn't an early A's game today. If there was, traffic was going to be a bear.

They were in luck. He followed the signs to the Oakland Coliseum BART station and parked the rental car in the first space he could find. "Come on."

They got fare tickets and headed for the nearest outdoor platform.

"Where are we going?" She turned to look at signs.

"Anywhere that leaves here the soonest."

She met his eyes. "Oh. Gotcha."

While they waited for the train, Clay tried to keep himself from fidgeting. His body felt taut like a guitar string wound too tightly, and he kept his eyes roving the platform, everywhere he could see, looking for any suspicious behavior. There were still a lot of people since morning rush hour was only just ending, but he didn't see Met and G.

Had they been far enough ahead of the tail?

There was a chance G would step onto the platform and start firing his gun any minute. Clay clenched his hands. He'd deal with that scenario if it happened. He had to focus on observing everything around him right now.

Which was how he was able to notice the man in the leather jacket.

Clay hadn't particularly singled him out when he stepped onto the platform, coolly walking down its length without looking at anyone, solely focused on his smartphone. But then Clay noted how his steps were too deliberate: he didn't slow, he just continued toward them.

Clay turned away from him, feigning disinterest. But he kept him in the corner of his eye.

It enabled to him to react a split second before the man grabbed his arm.

Clay sent an elbow back into the man's nose. He jerked backward and toppled to the ground, more out of surprise than from the blow.

"Oh, sorry about that," Clay said loudly. "I didn't see you." He quickly went to his knees and snatched the man's gun from the shoulder holster under his jacket before he could react.

As he paused to stow the gun in his waistband, the man recovered enough to grab Clay by the collar and slam his forehead into Clay's face.

Clay saw darkness and light. And pain. He could almost see his own pain in front of his eyes like stars. He dimly registered a blow to his torso, followed by distressed cries from someone nearby.

His vision cleared and he saw people backing away from him and the man. He was on his side, curled up as the man was quickly getting to his feet, probably to aim a kick at Clay's head.

Clay lashed out with his legs in a move that brought his opponent crashing down to the ground again. Before the man could regain his bearings, Clay leaped for him and caught him in a guillotine choke hold.

"Clay!" Joslyn shouted. But it wasn't a cry of worry. It was to get his attention.

He looked up at her and she pointed. There were two trains approaching, one on this side, and one on the platform on the other side of the track.

He understood her silent plea. "Go!" he told her.

She ran, heading for the stairs to the other platform.

The man twisted, fighting the choke hold, but Clay didn't let up. After another few seconds, the man passed out. Clay leaped to his feet and followed Joslyn. Every footstep jarred his bruised stomach, but he sprinted for all he was worth.

He'd only gotten to the stairs when he skidded to a halt. Joslyn was struggling with a second man who had both her wrists in his hands. She kept him so occupied that he didn't even see

Clay come up behind him and knock him down with a blow to the back of his neck.

They raced to the other platform. The train had already arrived and people were filing inside. They found seats next to each other, and Clay twisted to look out the window, surveying the area. He hoped the train wasn't one of those that would wait too long before leaving the station.

Or even worse, he hoped someone hadn't called security and they'd be here to drag Clay off the train. Clay scanned the crowd, and most people were ignoring them, some reading books or looking at their smartphones. One or two people saw him looking at them and glanced away quickly. Were they embarrassed to be caught staring or was it nervousness because they'd seen Clay fight with those two men?

Then the doors *whooshed* shut, and Clay found he was able to breathe again. Beside him, Joslyn gave a sigh of relief, too. When the train started, he slumped in his seat.

"I didn't consider them sending a different team to follow us," Clay said. "They must have sent them from San Francisco or Los Angeles once they were able to track the rental car."

"How many resources do these people have?" Joslyn said.

"I wasn't thinking." Clay pounded his fist into his knee, and the injured tendons twanged. "I underestimated them."

"You couldn't have known," Joslyn said. She'd jumped a little when he hit his knee, but her voice was calm.

"I've worked with men like them enough to have guessed what they were capable of." Then he discreetly reached unto his waistband and passed her the man's gun. "Took this off the guy with the jacket."

She quickly hid it in her purse. "Let me call Liam." Joslyn pulled out a cell phone.

Last night, as they were driving out of Phoenix, Joslyn had called the O'Neill Agency to explain the situation. Liam was supposed to meet them at a parking garage in order to help them switch cars, but that was going to be harder to do now that they had to rely on public transportation.

"Got it." Joslyn ended the call and turned to Clay. "We're heading south right now, so we'll have to get off at the next station and backtrack, then catch a bus. But Liam is going to meet us at a small bus station up north on the way to Sonoma."

Several hours later, they finally arrived at the designated bus station, both of them weary. Joslyn had used the ride to catch up on sleep, and despite wanting to stay alert, Clay also slept.

The station was an unmanned park-n-ride, and when he exited the bus, Joslyn immediately waved to a man leaning against a green Grand Cherokee. He was long and lean, with his brown hair in a buzz cut that emphasized his wide jaw and prominent cheekbones. Next to him was a young Filipino woman who smiled at Joslyn warmly and another man with a widow's peak above blue eyes.

"Clay, this is my boss, Liam O'Neill," Joslyn said, introducing the man with the buzz cut, who shook Clay's hand in a firm grip. "This is my other boss, and Liam's girlfriend, Elisabeth Aday, and this is Liam's older brother, Shaun O'Neill." The man with the widow's peak shook Clay's hand.

"Thank you for protecting Joslyn," Elisabeth said to him. "She means a lot to us."

"No, she doesn't," Shaun said, a twinkle in his eyes. "She's a brat, aren't you?" He tried to grab Joslyn in a headlock.

She squealed and twisted out of his way. "You're such a bully, Shaun."

Shaun looked at his hands as if surprised she'd gotten free. "Liam must have taught you some moves, girl."

"Of course I did," Liam said. "I'm not letting you push her around like you did with the rest of us."

"I was toughening you boys up," Shaun said defensively, but with an answering grin.

The horseplay made Clay smile, but at the same time there was an ache in his chest. He'd never had a brother to joke with like this. But it was more than that—all four of them were comfortable with each other, shared the ease and love between friends.

He'd lost any friends he'd had in the mob when he went to prison, and for the past couple years he'd been so focused on getting his life back that he'd kept himself aloof, even from the guys at his gym. He remembered the camaraderie he'd had in Chicago and missed it. He was tired of being alone.

"You two cavemen can beat your chests some other time," Elisabeth said. Her expression sobered. "We've got other problems."

Clay's shoulders tensed. "What kinds of problems?"

"Our friend, Detective Carter, gave us a call because he recognized Joslyn," Elisabeth said. "Someone on the BART platform caught you on video beating up a couple guys. The police are looking for you."

This day just kept getting better and better.

"But Clay was protecting me," Joslyn said.

"We know, it's actually on the video," Elisabeth said. "There's a one-second clip of Clay choking out one guy in a leather jacket, then rushing to hit the other one who'd grabbed you."

"Look, Detective Carter with the Sonoma police is a good friend," Liam said. "We'll go with you to talk to him and get it sorted out."

Clay's first instinct was to run. His past had conditioned him to steer clear of the cops. But he couldn't help Fiona if he was being pursued by the authorities for something that was pure self-defense.

Then again, he couldn't help Fiona if he was in jail, either.

Joslyn was looking at him, worry in her amber-colored eyes. She was probably remembering Phoenix and the problems they'd had there. He didn't want to drag her into any more trouble. And even if he was in jail, she'd continue to look for Fiona.

Clay sighed, then nodded. "Let's go. I guess it's better than waiting for the police to come looking for us."

"Nothing will happen to you," Liam said quietly. "We'll make sure of that."

Clay should have been suspicious of his reassurance, but somehow the way he said it made Clay feel he could trust him. He'd had to survive on his instincts, both in Chicago and in prison, and so he trusted them now, too.

"Before we go to the Sonoma police station, can we stop at my apartment first?" Joslyn said. "We got pictures of the two men in Phoenix. I want to run them through that facial-recognition program I've been working on with Jane Lawton."

"You can give that to Detective Carter to run through their own similar program," Liam said.

"But mine crawls through the web to find photos of subjects on social media, news and blogs. I can find information on them that the police may not have. The process will take a while so I want to start it as soon as possible."

"We may be at the station for some time," Elisabeth said thoughtfully. "Maybe it would be good to start the program running now."

"What about my rental car?" Joslyn asked.

"My wife and I will pick it up from the BART station and return it for you," Shaun said.

"And don't think I've forgotten that you still need to debrief me on what's been going on," Liam said affectionately to Joslyn. He gave her a brotherly hug—the kind that made her groan in pain—as he lifted her off the ground. "All the stuff you left out of our phone conversations because you didn't want to worry us."

"I think I'd rather talk to the police," Joslyn groused, but Liam and Elisabeth were smiling.

They drove to a new development outside of Sonoma, Clay and Joslyn with Elisabeth in the Cherokee, and Liam with his brother in a Suburban. Clay scanned the cars around them the entire time. He knew he was probably being paranoid, but he'd rather be safe than sorry. Joslyn's apartment complex was across the street from a small lake park. There were several buildings, each holding four to six units, with lots of walkways and trees in between.

Joslyn's apartment was on the second floor of a four-unit building. As Joslyn, Clay and Elisabeth walked up the wooden flight of stairs, Clay could clearly hear Joslyn's neighbor through an open window. "Hello? Naomi? Naomi?" The elderly woman's voice was high-pitched. "I can't hear you. Take me off speakerphone. Haven't you learned to use your phone yet?"

"Mrs. Zachariah," Joslyn explained. "She's a little hard of hearing."

Clay leaned against the wall next to Joslyn's front door while she dug out her key. "Where are Liam and Shaun?" Clay asked Elisabeth.

"Waiting in the car." Elisabeth rolled her eyes. "Probably listening to a game on the radio."

"Naomi, what's all that noise in the background?" Mrs. Zachariah said. "It sounds like a truck driving through your living room."

"Here it is." Joslyn found her key and unlocked her door.

The old woman continued, "I swear, it's as bad as that ruckus I heard earlier this morning."

Clay reacted purely on instinct. He had no reason to think the noise Mrs. Zachariah had heard had anything to do with Joslyn's apartment, but his arm whipped out to wrap around her even as he put his body in between her and her front door, which she'd pushed open a crack.

He heard the roar of the explosion, then nothing. The door flew at them and he raised his arm to protect his head.

Pain shattered his left arm, stabbing up his shoulder. Stars rained across his vision, and then everything went dark.

EIGHT

She would be dead if not for him.

Joslyn stood next to the window in Clay's hospital room, letting the spring sunshine warm her. She was too cold.

She'd felt cold ever since waking up on the floor of the hallway outside her apartment, Clay's body sprawled on top of her, splinters of her door all around them, plaster raining on her head. She hadn't been able to hear a thing, and white smoke had misted everything in front of her dazed vision.

She'd rolled Clay over, shouted at him even though she could barely hear her own voice. He'd been unconscious but breathing. Elisabeth had been thrown a few feet away and had sustained a cut across her cheek.

Another bomb, like the one at Fiona's house. When the men realized she was going to Sonoma, they must have gone straight to her apartment to rig it to explode.

She shivered. Too much had happened in the past day and a half. She felt as if she was going to fly apart.

Not yet. She couldn't go to pieces yet. Fiona was still out there. These men wouldn't stop trying to hurt them. She had to focus.

She felt too helpless, too frustrated, too out of control. She wanted to know what she should do to make all this stop, to find Fiona. Maybe she should have suspected a bomb at her apartment and been more cautious—after all, someone had rigged Fiona's house. She felt she should have been able to predict more of their opponents' moves than she had.

And here she was, watching over an unconscious man who had thrown himself on top of her to shield her from the blast, unable to do anything else besides wait for him to wake up.

She pulled out her wallet, a new one she'd bought at the mall in Arizona, where she'd put the little bachelor's button flower that he'd tucked into her hair. It seemed stupid to save it, pressed between two dollar bills, but she hadn't wanted to toss it. She remembered the tenderness of his fingers as they touched her face.

She closed the wallet and put it away, glancing at Clay's still form. She felt useless. She'd been almost panicked when she saw he'd been knocked unconscious. There hadn't been anything she could do. She and Elisabeth had waited beside Clay for the ambulance while Liam and Shaun had helped her neighbors, including Mrs. Zachariah, who had been injured when part of the wall exploded into her living room. How had he known about the bomb? Or maybe God had somehow tipped him off, protecting them all. *Thank You, Lord.* She hadn't stopped praying that since they'd gotten to the hospital.

"Hey, beautiful." Clay's voice was a raspy whisper, but Joslyn was glad to hear it at all.

She moved to the chair beside his bed. "How are you feeling?"

"Like I was in an explosion."

"Don't be a wise guy."

"I know a girl who'd shoot me if I was ever that." He smiled weakly at her. Part of the door had clocked him across his brow and he had a magnificent black eye. "Are you okay?"

"I'm fine." Just a few minor cuts and bruises. "You're the one with the broken arm and the shiner the size of a grapefruit."

"Really? I want to see." He looked around for a mirror.

"There's no way I can carry you to the bathroom just to look at your black eye."

He suddenly sobered. "Was anyone else hurt?" he asked in a low voice.

"Elisabeth has a minor concussion, and my neighbors had some injuries, but the doctor says they'll all be okay."

He frowned. "I should have predicted their next move. I should have guessed about the bomb."

"I was just telling myself the same thing."

His eyes bored into hers. "But I worked with guys like that for years. I got to know how they think, how they work. I should have been smarter."

"You saved my life," she said softly, and took his hand.

He squeezed her hand tightly, his eyes intent, his face pale. "I'm glad you're all right."

His fingers had calluses, probably from working out at his gym, and his hand was warm compared to hers. His touch was reassuring and strong, as if he could give her part of his strength and make her into a more confident, capable person. She realized he did that to her just by being near her. She wanted to sit here, holding his hand, for another few years.

There was a knock at the open door, and Liam and Detective Carter came into the room. "Good, you're awake," Liam said. "Clay, this is Detective Horatio Carter."

Detective Carter shook Clay's hand. "Thank you for saving our girl, here."

Joslyn rolled her eyes. "I feel like I have a million uncles. I'm twenty-five, not twelve."

Liam leaned over and said in a mock whisper to Clay, "She'll be grateful, eventually."

"I am very grateful," Joslyn said. "You, Liam O'Neill, are being annoying."

"Be nice to me. I'm your boss."

"So fire me. Elisabeth will simply hire me back."

Liam frowned at her. "It irritates me when you're right."

Detective Carter cleared his throat. "Children..."

Joslyn smiled at him. She had gotten to know him very well when she first came to Sonoma, and while the detective had a gravelly voice and steel-gray eyes that could be very intimidating, he was a softie at heart and he really did care about her.

"How are you feeling?" Liam asked Clay.

He opened his mouth, eyed Joslyn, then said, "Fine. Relatively speaking."

"Arm hurt too much?"

His left forearm had been put into a splint and then immobilized against his body in a sling. He shrugged. "It's okay. Timing could be better," he added with a grimace.

"When is it ever a good time to break an arm?" she said.

His eyes were serious. "I don't like being sidelined just when it seems the danger's getting worse for us."

They had to do something. They had to find Fiona and stop this threat. She didn't want to think about how she'd feel if he were more gravely injured.

"Did you bring Elisabeth's computer?" she asked Liam.

He unslung his backpack and handed her a laptop. "Why this one?"

"It's one of the only computers that can access my encrypted cloud drive." Her desktop had been destroyed in the explosion.

"What encrypted cloud drive?" Detective Carter asked.

"All my computer files are backed up onto a secure cloud server. I learned that trick from Elisabeth," Joslyn said. "But I did one better and made it so that only certain computers can access the drive. Elisabeth's laptop is one of them."

"You're going to run that facial-recognition program?" Clay asked.

"That's already running on one of Elisabeth's computers at her apartment," she said. "We set that up while we were waiting for you to get your beauty rest."

Clay gave her a sour look.

"I'm guessing that whoever rigged my apartment tried to break into my computer, but I have a security program that turns on the camera and starts shooting video. The video file is saved on my cloud drive."

"Are you saying you may have gotten a video of the people who rigged your apartment?" Detective Carter's red-gold brows rose toward his thinning hairline.

"Maybe. I'll have to access the drive to find out."

"I'll have a chat with Mr. Ashton while you're doing that," the detective said.

"I'll check on Elisabeth." Liam nodded to all of them and left to go to her room, which was on the floor below.

Joslyn had built an extensive security protocol to log into her cloud drive, so it took her a few minutes. Detective Carter talked to Clay not only about the explosion but also about the events on the BART platform.

He nodded as he finished taking notes.

"Did the video show what happened to the two guys?"

Detective Carter shook his head. "We've sent out a general request to ask for any other video that was shot, but it'll take a few days if we do get anything. And Joslyn gave us the gun you took off the guy with the jacket, so we're in the process of tracing that now."

"We can give you the pictures of the two guys in Phoenix, too."

"I got those from Joslyn already," the detective said.

"I've got even better pictures of them," Joslyn said.

"You do? Where?" Clay asked.

She swiveled the laptop around so Clay and the detective could see the video she'd pulled up from her cloud drive. As she suspected, someone had tried to access her computer and failed, but not before it shot a few minutes of video as they tried to break her login code.

The video showed the man named Met from the Mexican restaurant parking lot, his curly head bent over her computer keyboard. He was snacking as he typed, and Joslyn would have been appalled at the potato chip crumbs on her desk if she hadn't known her computer would be incinerated in a few hours.

Behind him, the man named G was walking back and forth, carrying various things apparently to the front door, although that wasn't visible in the angle from the camera. At one point he turned to Met and said, "Aren't you done yet?"

The camera captured high definition video, so it got a good shot of his face as he turned directly to the computer screen.

"It's not as easy as you think," Met grumbled. He upended his bag of chips, which was empty, and tossed it to the ground. Then he grabbed another bag of treats from his pocket and ripped it open with his teeth before reaching in with his mouth to grab a snack. Joslyn recognized it. It was lemon peel candy, and the bag was from Kandie's, a Chinese candy store in Los Angeles that Fiona had often gone to. She'd always brought a bag to class, but Joslyn didn't care for Chinese candy and hadn't eaten any when she'd offered.

After a few moments, Met gave a disgusted noise. "Forget it, I can't get into this. Are you done yet?"

"Another minute."

Met left the computer, and after a few seconds of showing Joslyn's empty chair, the video ended.

Detective Carter frowned. "Could I get a copy of that?"

"Sure. I'll share it on my public cloud drive and email you the link."

He nodded. "I'll also request the report of the explosion from the Arizona police. Maybe there's something to link the two explosions."

"Thanks, Detective."

He smiled and cupped her cheek in his weathered hand. "I'm just glad you're all right." He then reached out to clasp Clay's shoulder. "Both of you."

Clay seemed a bit embarrassed by the gesture, but bemused, as well. What had it been like to grow up with a stepfather like Martin? Had their relationship always been this bad?

The detective's cell phone rang. "Sorry, I have to take this." He rose and left the room.

"Could you play the video again?" Clay asked. "What was that candy he was eating?"

So he'd noticed that, too. She played the video and stopped it on a good shot of the bag.

"That's lemon peel," Clay said.

"Did Fiona buy Chinese candies in Chicago, too?"

"There were a couple stores in the city that sold the kinds she liked."

"I know that store." Joslyn nodded to the bag. "It's in Los Angeles. Fiona always brought candy to class. Her favorite was—"

"—Li hing mui." A smile hovered around Clay's mouth. "I thought it was okay but it wasn't my favorite."

Joslyn made a face. "I didn't like it at all." It had been a combination of salty and extremely sour with an unusual spice mixed in that didn't appeal to her.

"Does the store have a website?"

Joslyn went online. Kandie's was a small family-run store near Chinatown.

Something about that was wrong. Joslyn pulled up a map of Los Angeles and figured out why. "I always assumed Kandie's was near Fiona's home, but that's nowhere near the place she rented." She pointed to the location on the map where Fiona's home had been, which was miles away, with heavy traffic areas in between.

Clay suddenly frowned fiercely. "That store is less than a block away from Martin's office building."

Surprised, Joslyn was silent a moment, trying to make that fact compute. "Are you sure?"

"It's right here." Clay pointed on the map.

"I know she was close with her father, but I didn't know she visited him at his office that often. She opened a new bag of candy every day. When she talked to me about meeting up with him, it was usually for dinner about once a month. Maybe she stocked up."

"Is the store even open in the evenings?" Clay asked.

Joslyn checked and found that the store closed at five. "We usually had class until five or six. Sometimes later if there was a lab."

"So Joslyn was visiting Martin during the day?"

"And she never mentioned it to me." That was unusual. Fiona had always seemed so open about her life. It hadn't seemed as though she was keeping secrets. But then again, she'd been sad and stressed the last few months before she left Los Angeles. She'd told Joslyn it was school, but what if it was something else, something she'd been hiding? Like her visits to her father during the day.

"Maybe that was just her favorite store for Chinese candy," Clay said. "She had one favorite store that was clear across Chicago, and she'd go once a month."

"No, she told me her favorite store was Garth's, which is in San Bernadino. Sometimes she'd show up with candy from there, but usually it was from

Kandie's. I always assumed Kandie's was closer to her home and more convenient for her."

"So this store, *near Martin's office*, was convenient for her? No. I can't believe she'd be involved in anything with Martin."

"It may have been something perfectly legitimate." Except that Fiona had kept the visits from Joslyn for some reason. That made it seem less likely that they were aboveboard.

"If those men are connected to Martin," Clay said, pointing to the picture of Met on the laptop screen, "and they rigged your house with explosives, that means they rigged Fiona's house, too. Martin tried to kill her."

Joslyn's heart blipped. "How could Martin try to kill his own daughter?"

"What other explanation is there?"

"We don't know for certain these men are connected to Martin. Just because of the candy…" But she couldn't think of any other reason Fiona would be in that section of Los Angeles other than to see Martin.

"We've been assuming the bomb at Fiona's house was meant to kill her," Clay said. "But maybe it was meant to prevent anyone else from finding her. Martin saw her just before she disappeared, but the house wasn't rigged until a day or two later, because her neighbor was able to get Fiona's dog out of her house without any problems."

"I see what you're saying. If Martin wanted to kill Fiona, he'd have rigged the house sooner."

"If that bomb in Phoenix wasn't meant for Fiona, that means the two guys after us only want to prevent us from finding her."

"So maybe Martin is trying to protect her. Maybe he knows where she is."

"Or maybe he's looking for her *and* trying to prevent anyone else from finding her," Clay said darkly.

"Do you really think he'd try to harm her?"

"No," he said slowly, "but I can believe that he needs her for something. The man is selfish to the core. Sometimes I was amazed he spared any emotion for Fiona at all."

Joslyn was saddened by the bitterness in his tone and what Martin must have done to him to make him so angry. She'd had such a good relationship with her own father, and she hadn't appreciated it until it was too late.

Grief closed her throat, and she had to take a few deep breaths before she could speak again. "If we don't know why Fiona disappeared, I don't know where to start looking for her."

"I thought you were going to look into what she was doing in Phoenix before she disappeared."

"I did, a little, but I really can't find anything," Joslyn said. "When she went to Phoenix, she was doing her best to stay off the grid. Her name was misspelled on her house rental agreement, and I thought it must have been some type of clerical error. But then I started looking into other things. She deliberately misspelled her name on her job application, her utilities, even the museum membership. It's not illegal, but it makes it harder for a skip tracer to find her."

"So if she was already trying to hide her identity when she went to Arizona," Clay said, "then there was something in Los Angeles that she was trying to get away from."

"That's what I'm thinking, too. I'll do some internet digging into what she was doing in LA."

"We should talk to her old roommates."

"I talked to them about a week ago on the phone. I know them a little from when Fiona was in school. But we only chatted briefly, because once I heard from them that Fiona had moved to Arizona, then I knew how to target my search."

"People are usually willing to tell you more than they intended to if you're face-to-face." He suddenly reached out to grab her hand. She hadn't even realized she was rubbing her scar.

"Don't rub it," he said.

"I didn't know I was," she mumbled. Even when she wanted to, she couldn't escape that reminder from Tomas. Or rather, from his gold ring.

"I know," he said. There was a brief silence, then he seemed to remember he was holding her hand, and released it. "When can I get out of here?"

"That's up to the doctor."

He stretched his neck. "I feel okay."

"The last thing I want is for you to mysteriously collapse while we're out looking for Fiona, just because we took you out of the hospital too early."

She'd been teasing, but the look he gave her was sober. "Fiona's out there. I can't rest easy until I know she's okay."

He was right. He had even more reason to be worried about Fiona than she did. "Let me go get a nurse. They did say they were going to cast your arm later today."

She got up and went into the hallway. There was a uniformed officer sitting outside the room, which was a surprise to her since it had been Shaun O'Neill doing guard duty earlier, but Detective Carter must have put the officer in his place. The man nodded to her as she passed.

She headed to the nurse's station …and froze.

Several yards ahead of her, waiting for the elevator, stood a man in a rumpled jacket that was too large for him. He didn't stand out from the people milling around him except for his dark curly hair and his unshaven face, which gave him a scruffy appearance.

He happened to turn in her direction.

His eyes fell on her, uninterested, as if he didn't recognize her. Then just the faintest hint of a smile appeared. The elevator door opened and he turned and walked nonchalantly inside.

It was Met.

NINE

It felt good for Clay to be doing something. Being stuck in the hospital, unable to search for Fiona, had driven him crazy with worry.

He stood outside the house where Fiona had rented a room, a seventies-style house in a Los Angeles suburb. While Joslyn rang the doorbell, his eyes roved around the quiet neighborhood. It was hard for him to remember he was in LA because this was a cozier area than any he'd lived in for the few years during his childhood when he'd been here with his mother, Martin and Fiona. They'd been in a more upscale part of the city since Martin's business had started booming around that time and appearances were everything.

But despite the deceptively sleepy street, he kept careful watch of every car, every pedestrian. He'd been incredibly frustrated yesterday when Joslyn had told him about seeing Met at the hospital. Just when she might have needed protection, he'd been holed up in a bed like an invalid.

The hospital hadn't been all bad. He'd stayed overnight for observation, but Joslyn had been in his room the entire time, whether sitting by his bed and talking to him, or off in the corner on her computer. Liam O'Neill and his brother Shaun had also visited, as well as a bandaged-up Elisabeth who'd said she looked worse than she felt. Clay had found out that Liam, Shaun and one of their other brothers, Brady, all trained at a local mixed martial arts gym in Sonoma, so they'd talked MMA for a while.

Surprisingly, he'd found himself opening up about how he wanted to go professional in MMA but couldn't because of a knee injury from his mob henchman days. He hadn't gotten good rehab and it was still weak and filled with scar tissue, and Liam had mentioned that he knew a good physical therapist in Sonoma who could help him with that.

It made him want to stay here.

Joslyn and her friends made him feel wanted. It was different from the friendships he had in Illinois. There was a level of genuine concern, a deeper sense of inner peace, in each of these people. He thought it had to do with what Liam had said before he left.

"I'll be praying for you."

The words came naturally to him, effortlessly,

as if he had a close, comfortable relationship with God. Which made Clay uncomfortable because he didn't have a great relationship with the Almighty, himself.

Other Christians he'd met had seemed judgmental, especially when they found out he'd been in prison, or if they heard him cussing. It was in the tightness of their smiles and the way they seemed to hold themselves apart from him. He hadn't wanted anything to do with them if that was how they treated others.

But Joslyn and her friends weren't like that. Even when he'd accidentally dropped some bad words, they hadn't flinched. They seemed to like him for who he was. They made him feel as if he was someone they wanted to get to know better.

They'd also arranged for new clothes for him, and a new car for him and Joslyn, borrowing it from a friend of Shaun's wife's sister, or something like that. It would make it harder for anyone to connect it with them.

They'd only said goodbye when the doctor and a nurse came in to cast his splinted arm, now that the swelling had gone down. The doctor had set it, then left the nurse to wrap the coated strips over it in a plaster cast. He'd go in for a fiberglass cast in a week. Liam and Elisabeth had driven partway down to Los Angeles alongside them in separate cars to make sure there wasn't anyone following them, before turning back to head to

Sonoma when it was obvious they weren't being tailed. It had been an extra precaution that Clay had appreciated.

The door to the house opened, and a young African-American woman peered out at the two of them. Then she smiled at Joslyn. "Hey, Joslyn! Did you find Fiona?"

"Hi, Anna. No, unfortunately."

"Oh, that's too bad." Anna looked again at Clay, and her eyes narrowed. "Wait a minute, are you Clay?"

"Fiona's brother, yeah."

"Oh, my gosh, you really do look exactly like her. I mean, I saw some photos of you, but they were from a few years ago. Come on in, both of you."

The house was inviting despite its age. It had had a fresh coat of paint recently, although the hardwood floors were full of nicks and scratches collected over the years. The living room was small and low-ceilinged, but neatly furnished with reupholstered chairs and a faded floral couch. There were various things scattered around, including a football, a softball bat, a basket of knitting, and a stack of books on a table.

"Sorry for the mess," Anna said. "It's Chuck's turn to clean the living room but he's been in the middle of finals this week."

"How many people live here?" Clay asked.

"There's four of us," Anna said. "We each have

a bedroom, and we share the cooking and cleaning chores. It makes it more affordable for us to live in this area."

"I'll bet." He'd never had to pay rent while living in LA, but he remembered the price of apartments in Chicago, which was much higher than the cheap cost of living in southern Illinois, where he was now.

"Want some coffee? I just made a fresh pot." Without waiting for an answer, Anna sailed out of the living room.

Clay eased himself into a large oak chair, while Joslyn sat next to him in a dainty antique-y looking thing with spindly legs.

"Here you go." Anna came in with a tray with three mugs of coffee, as well as spoons, creamer, and sugar. "Chuck says I'm a terrible hostess, so be sure to tell him what I did for you, okay?" She winked at Joslyn. "Are you done with your master's yet?"

"I'm taking my last semester up in Sonoma," Joslyn said. "How about you?"

They chatted for a few minutes about themselves. Anna was interested in Clay since Fiona mentioned him, but not much about him, to her roommates. He was also grateful when some of Anna's questions were too probing and Joslyn smoothly interjected with comments that distracted the other woman's train of thought.

Finally Anna said, "So you didn't find Fiona in

Arizona? I'm not sure what else we can tell you. She was pretty tight-lipped about why she was moving there. Do you think she's in trouble?"

"We really don't know," Joslyn said. "You didn't notice her buying anything special before she moved out?"

"No. You know Fiona—she's all computers and candy. I don't know how she can eat so much sugar and not gain an ounce." Anna sighed.

At that moment, there was a key in the front door, then a young Asian woman appeared. She spotted Joslyn and grinned. "Hey, Joslyn! I didn't get to see you when you came by last time." She put down her backpack and gave Joslyn a hug.

"Mariella! I'd heard you'd moved in here. How are you doing?"

She rolled her eyes. "I just keep telling myself, I'm almost done, and everything will stop being so crazy once I graduate." Her eye fell on Clay. "Are you Clay? You look so much like Fiona."

"I get that a lot." He shook her hand.

"I'm Mariella. I was in the same master's degree program as Joslyn and Fiona. Does this mean you didn't find Fiona? We've been worried."

"We're hoping to find out more about why she left LA," Joslyn said. "We think it might have to do with why she disappeared."

"I wasn't living here when Fiona was, but Anna would know," Mariella said.

"We were all shocked when she said she was

going," Anna said. "She left within a week of telling us, although she'd paid up her rent through the quarter."

"Did she do anything weird?" Joslyn asked.

"Aside from packing so quickly? Nope," Anna said.

"Oh, but…" Mariella said, "we have a box of hers that I found a few months ago in the attic. She accidentally left it behind, and since we didn't know how to get in touch with her…"

"Oh, that's right," Anna said. "I'd forgotten about that. Did you want to take the box with you?"

"Definitely," Joslyn said.

"Is it heavy?" Clay asked.

"I'm not sure," Mariella said. "I didn't lift it. I just shoved it to one side after I realized it was Fiona's."

"I'll go up to get it." He rose to his feet.

Unlike the large attics of Victorian houses, this attic was barely a crawl space. It was a bit awkward with one arm in a cast, but Clay made his way across rafters draped in dust until he found a bunch of boxes against the side. Mariella had scrawled "Fiona" across the box she'd found, so it was easy for him to see it and drag it out of the attic. He lowered it to Mariella's and Joslyn's waiting hands, then dropped down from the access hole, which was in Chuck's closet.

Mariella and Joslyn both coughed at the dust

kicked up into the air from the box. "Chuck probably won't even notice the dust," Mariella said, glancing around at Chuck's messy room with distaste. "Still, I'll offer to help him clean later."

"I'll carry this outside to knock off the dust," Clay said. He hefted the box, which clinked as if there were china plates inside.

On the landing of the stairs was a narrow window that looked out to the street in front, and he happened to glance out. Or maybe it was the movement out front that caught his eye. Either way, he paused.

Met and G had just exited a black sedan. G reached into his jacket and pulled out a gun.

Joslyn was following Clay down the stairs when she saw him look out the window and freeze. And just that intent expression on his face made her entire body tense.

Suddenly he was shoving the dusty box into her arms. "Call the police. No matter what happens, don't come out of the house until the police arrive, do you hear me?" And then he launched himself down the rest of the stairs and out the front door.

"What's going on?" Mariella asked.

"Call the police, right now," Joslyn said. She rushed to the window and looked out, and at first she couldn't see anything. She shifted the box so she could lean closer to the window and look down.

Met and G were in the process of sneaking around the side of the house when Clay hurled himself at G.

Joslyn set the box down on the landing and pulled her firearm from her flashbang holster. Mariella, who was on her cell phone with the 9-1-1 operator, stared at her with wide eyes. She stuttered as she gave the address of the house.

Joslyn ran downstairs and locked the front door. She ran into the empty living room, where she could look out the window to the side and front yards.

Clay rolled around on the grass with G, struggling to gain control of a gun. Joslyn's heart thudded against the base of her throat. But Met... where was Met? He wasn't in the strip of grass that ran along the side of the house. She peered out the window and saw that the gate that separated the front from the backyard was cracked open.

Joslyn raced to the back door of the house. Was it locked? She guessed so—after all, this was LA. She arrived in the kitchen in time to see the doorknob jiggle. The knob was locked, but the deadbolt wasn't. She slammed her weight against the door and threw the deadbolt. Then she rolled out of the way, to the wall on the side of the door.

She was just in time. Met shot a round through the door where she'd been standing only a split second before. Through the doorway into the hallway, she saw someone duck into the living room at the same time she heard a woman's squeal.

Met began throwing his weight against the back door.

Joslyn grabbed the heavy oak breakfast table and tipped it on its end with a thud that made the floor shake. She dragged it so that the top faced the back door and her back was to the hallway.

Behind her, she saw Mariella peek out from behind the doorframe of the living room.

"Are you all right?" Joslyn whispered.

Mariella nodded.

"Where's Anna?"

"In her room."

"Get into the second floor bathroom and lock the door," Joslyn told her. "Then both of you get into the tub." She'd used the bathroom there a couple times in the past, and knew the heavy porcelain would protect them from any stray bullets.

Mariella darted across the hallway and pounded up the stairs.

"I know you're in there, Joslyn," Met said through the door. His voice was oily, confident. "We have Clay. Give yourself up and we won't hurt him."

She only had to stall them until the police arrived. But what if they killed Clay before that happened?

But if she left the house, they'd take both her and Clay. They might hurt Mariella and Anna, too.

Then Clay's voice sounded from behind the back door, "She's not in there. I came alone."

"I know you're lying," Met said calmly to Clay.

Then Clay's voice shot out in a cry of pain.

Joslyn's hands tightened around her weapon. She forced herself to breathe, to relax. She had to stay calm, stay focused.

"Joslyn, come out or we'll send Clay here to his step-daddy in little pieces."

What? Did that mean they weren't working for Martin?

Clay must have realized that, too, because he gave a low laugh. "He's not going to care about me. Your boss doesn't have all his facts right."

Moving quietly and staying low, Joslyn crept from behind the table until she was behind the sink. She slowly rose until she could see outside the window that hung right over the sink.

G held Clay's arms behind his back. There were fresh cuts on Clay's face, and his hair was a wild blond mess around his head. Clay's left shoulder was hitched a little higher than the other, and she wondered if he'd reinjured his broken arm in its cast.

Met was hissing something to G, obviously displeased about something. Maybe they had expected to take them by surprise, which wouldn't have allowed Joslyn and the others time to call the police or barricade themselves inside the house. Thanks to Clay, they hadn't been blindsided.

Met's face was red. He pointed his gun directly at Clay's bent head, and Joslyn couldn't breathe.

Met shouted, "Joslyn, you come out right now, or I swear I'll—"

Suddenly Clay snapped his head backward and clocked G full in the face. The man grunted and Clay pulled free.

Met's gun went off.

Joslyn's heart went into overdrive. She gripped her weapon, ready to fire out the window at them, but then realized there was no blood. Clay had staggered backward but was still standing. Met had missed.

Clay slammed his right elbow at G's face, but the man blocked it with his arm and countered with a fist to Clay's side. He grunted, but recovered quickly and twisted full around to tackle G to the ground. They rolled in the grass and weeds of the backyard while Met aimed his gun at the two of them, looking for a shot.

Then she heard the wail of sirens.

Met swore, then started running toward the side gate. "G, come on!"

G managed to get to his feet, but Clay clung to his legs. G kicked out at Clay, who released him. Then the man ran after Met.

Joslyn unlocked the back door and headed outside cautiously, her weapon at the ready, but the backyard was empty except for Clay. She ran to where he lay on the ground.

"Are you all right? Your arm…"

"I'm fine." He was breathing heavily. He winced a little as he sat up.

The sirens were deafening, now, and they stopped right outside the front of the house. Had they managed to catch Met and G or had the thugs gotten away?

Armed police officers came into the backyard through the side gate, shouting orders she couldn't quite understand. Too late, she wondered if she ought to have reholstered her firearm. She laid the gun down on the ground and put her arms up.

"Did you see the two men who were running away?" she said. "One had curly hair, the other one had short, brown hair and was taller…"

"Hey!" Clay shouted.

An officer yanked her arms behind her back. She heard the clink of handcuffs just before cold steel bit into her wrists.

TEN

They were wasting time. Joslyn jerked angrily at her handcuffs. Fiona was out there running from dangerous men like Met and G, and Joslyn was still sitting on the front porch with her hands cuffed behind her back.

Anna and Mariella had told the officers what had happened, several times, in fact. Sometimes talking both at the same time, which didn't help matters. The officers had been about to let Joslyn go when they ran Clay's ID and saw his record. Unsure what to do about his "associate," they'd left Joslyn in cuffs.

Thankfully, Clay had called Liam as soon as he could, but even when he did that, one of the officers had demanded to know who he was calling.

"Her boss," Clay said brusquely, and the officer frowned and moved away.

Clay had been on the phone almost constantly for the past hour, but she couldn't make out who he was talking to. That might be because there was at least one policeman near her at all times.

Then one of the officers in charge got a phone call. His voice became crisper, more deferential. "Yes, sir…no, sir…"

Finally he disconnected the call and approached her, a thundercloud expression on his face. And then he unlocked her handcuffs. "You're free to go," he muttered.

Her shoulders were sore from being restrained for so long, and she rubbed them. "Could I please have my ID and my conceal-and-carry license?"

The lawman grudgingly handed them to her, and then she added, "And my firearm?"

He hesitated.

Clay was suddenly there, his cell phone in his hand, although he wasn't talking into it. "Is she being arrested? Charged with anything?"

"No."

"Then give her back her firearm."

The officer handed her the gun. Clay helped her to her feet and they went back into the house.

In the foyer, Clay handed her the phone. "Here. It's Detective Carter."

That's who he had been talking to? Joslyn took the cell phone. "Hello?"

"Joslyn, are you all right?" Detective Carter's gravelly voice was music to her ears.

She had to fight an unexpected tightness in

her throat. "I'm fine. Are you the one who called that officer?"

"No, that was a friend of mine." There was humor in his voice. "I called in a favor."

"I'm sorry you had to do that for me."

"You're worth it."

She wiped away a tear. "Thanks."

"I'll see you later."

She disconnected the call and handed it back to Clay.

He took it, then folded her in his arms.

It felt wonderful. He was solid, warm, comforting. She smelled stalwart cedar, uplifting citrus and calming musk. She could relax, rely on his strength, let his presence chase away the stress and humiliation of the past hour.

She leaned back, but kept her hand on his chest. Without looking at him, she said, "Thank you."

His hand covered hers on his chest and squeezed. "You're worth it."

She tried to remember all the reasons she couldn't let herself get closer to him, all the ways he reminded her of Tomas, but it was useless. All she knew was the comfort of his hand holding hers, the steadiness of his heartbeat under her fingers.

She had to focus on Fiona.

She stepped away from him.

Even if there wasn't all this crazy danger surrounding him, she couldn't consider anything deeper with Clay. He wasn't a Christian, he lived in Illinois. He was strong, powerful, confident.

She was too afraid.

She hadn't made right choices before, and she'd lost *everything*. Her father, her home. Her baby.

She was rebuilding her life and she wouldn't risk it. Not again.

Joslyn moved into the living room, where Anna and Mariella were sitting and talking.

"They finally let you go," Anna said. "I just made more coffee. You want something to eat, too?"

"I'm fine, thanks," Joslyn said. "I'm so sorry about all this."

"It's not your fault," Mariella said. "I wish they'd caught those goons."

"Who were they?" Anna asked.

"We don't know," Clay said from behind Joslyn. His voice was neutral, normal-sounding. "But we saw them in Phoenix, too."

"They're after you because of Fiona?" Mariella asked.

"We just don't know. That's why we're trying to find out everything we can about Fiona before she moved to Phoenix."

Mariella nodded toward the coffee table. "We put the box there for you."

"Would you mind looking through it with us?" Joslyn asked. "There might be some things you can tell us about the stuff inside."

"Sure." Anna leaped to her feet.

The largest thing in the box was a spun glass ornament in shades of red, blue, orange and yellow. When Mariella held it up, the light shone through and cast the colors upon the walls.

"Oooh," Anna said.

"I know that," Clay said. "It's from an artisan's shop in Lake Tahoe. Fiona loved looking in there whenever we went to Tahoe on vacation."

"I can see why," Mariella said, turning the ornament in her hands.

There were a few framed photographs. One was of Fiona holding up a huge largemouth bass.

"That's from a houseboating trip we took. Whoever caught the smallest bass had to cook for a month," Anna said, snickering. "Chuck bragged the most and lost."

Another photo was of Fiona and Joslyn in evening dresses in front of the Zeddmore Museum of Art. "I had forgotten about this," Joslyn said. "Fiona got exclusive tickets to the opening for a new exhibit of Japanese art, so I went with her."

Another photo, this one in a faded Mickey Mouse frame, was of Fiona as a young girl with another little girl, the two of them wearing identical Mickey Mouse T-shirts and Goofy hats. A teenaged Clay was behind them, flanked by two older women, and looking bored. One of the women looked exactly like Clay and Fiona.

"Is that your mom?" Joslyn asked him.

He nodded. "We had season passes to Disneyland and went at least once a month. We got to know a lot of other season pass holders like Hannah and Amelia." He pointed to the other woman and the little girl.

There were also a bunch of paperback books in the box, all best-selling romances. They looked fairly new and most had price stickers on the back from the store where Fiona had bought them.

"She has a thing about cracks on the spine," Mariella said. "It never looks like she reads her books. The only way you can tell is if the pages aren't quite tight enough to be brand-new."

There was also a beautiful seashell, which looked as if it had come out of the ocean because it wasn't lacquered or polished.

"Did Fiona do any deep-sea diving?" Joslyn asked.

Mariella and Anna shrugged. "Not as far as I know," Mariella said.

There was also a ratty pair of house slippers, made out of woven bamboo strips for the footbed and stuffed cotton fabric tubes for straps.

"She wore those in the house all the time," Anna said.

"I remember," Joslyn said. "I didn't think about it before, but they look Japanese, don't they?"

"Yeah, they look like my grandma's house slippers," Mariella said. "I'm a quarter Japanese."

"She didn't have those in Chicago," Clay said.

"Did she have this in Chicago?" Joslyn held up a Chicago Cubs sweatshirt that was brand-new— it even still had the tags on the label. "I thought she was a die-hard Dodgers fan."

"Yup." Clay grinned. "I bought it for her just to annoy her."

They had gone through the entire contents of the box. Joslyn looked down at all the items on the table, but couldn't see how any of it pointed to what Fiona had been up to while she was Los Angeles, apart from her schoolwork.

"Do you know if she did anything outside of school?" Joslyn asked Anna and Mariella. "Something without you guys or her other friends?"

Mariella tilted her head as she thought. "Sometimes she'd go to art museums by herself. Actually, she might have gone by herself more often in the months before she moved away."

"She didn't always tell us where she went," Anna said. "We usually assumed she was at school or a museum."

"Or getting candy," Mariella said with a smile.

Joslyn looked over each item. "She didn't go to Disneyland?"

"Maybe once or twice, but it was usually with us or other friends," Anna said.

Joslyn fingered the shell. "How about on any vacations?"

"No…" Anna said slowly. "But she did go on a short trip once. I happened to wake up and see her leaving the house with a small roller bag and a messenger bag over her shoulder."

Joslyn hadn't known about this. "Do you remember when this was?"

"I don't remember exactly, it's been so long... summertime, maybe?"

Probably during the short summer break in between semesters for their degree program.

Anna continued, "She didn't say where, but she mentioned it was a trip with her dad. She was only gone a couple days."

"She went on another trip with her dad," Mariella said. "It was winter sometime, and it was only for a couple days, like over the weekend. I only found out about it because she was having car problems and she needed a ride to the airport."

Joslyn hadn't known anything about Fiona taking trips with Martin, but then again, he was her father and he had the money to be able to take her on a vacation anytime he wanted.

"So with four of you in the house," Clay said, "would you notice if she were gone a couple days at a time? Could she have taken more than just those two trips?"

"Yeah, she could have," Anna said. "Our schedules were completely different. Sometimes we'd go for days without seeing each other."

Joslyn felt they'd discovered something important. What were these trips Fiona had taken with

Martin? Had she gone on more than one of them? Where had she gone—and why?

"What was she wearing when she left on those trips?" she asked Anna and Mariella,

"A summer dress," Mariella said.

Anna said, "Jeans and a jacket."

"She could have been wearing those things because of the weather here, or it could be because of the weather where she was going," Joslyn said thoughtfully. "It's hard to know."

"Martin's the key," Clay said. "When those two thugs mentioned Martin, they obviously didn't know him. I'm guessing they're not working for him. Maybe the reason she's gone has to do with these trips Martin took with her. So he might be protecting her after all."

"Like I thought," Joslyn said. "So where would Martin take Fiona to protect her?"

Clay held up the glass ornament. "I think I know."

Clay hadn't driven down this road around Lake Tahoe in years, but landmarks here and there popped out at him familiarly—the Spangler Café, where Fiona bullied him into going because she liked their muffins, the eight-foot-tall carved grizzly bear at the entrance to a rustic motel, a formation of rocks just off the shore that was glimpsed through a break in the trees. Joslyn had driven most of the way there, but he'd taken over in Tahoe.

The landmarks and attractions reminded him of his time here with Fiona. He was certain she had to be here. Would she be glad to see him? He couldn't help a slight niggling of nervousness.

"How do you know Bobby will even be at his cabin?" Joslyn asked. Bobby was Martin's cousin and a self-proclaimed mountain man. His secluded cabin would be the perfect hideout for Fiona.

Joslyn looked out the passenger-side window of the car at the redwoods and firs edging the lake. "If it's his vacation home..."

"It was when Fiona and I came to visit," Clay said, "but he moved up here to live permanently around the time Martin divorced my mom and she and I left Los Angeles."

Her soft gaze made him uncomfortable, as if she could see all the hurt he'd felt at the time. "Martin had custody of Fiona?"

"He sued for custody and won because Mom could only get low-paying jobs to support us." He remembered her working two jobs at once to pay for their tiny apartment. It had been the reason they'd left California.

"But didn't Martin pay child support? Alimony?"

Clay shrugged, but it hid the burning anger in his chest. "His lawyer was better than Mom's. He barely paid enough to support her, and none for me since I wasn't his biological son. She'd been out of the workforce for so long, she had a hard time finding a job."

"That's awful," she breathed.

"That's Martin," Clay said.

There was silence for a while, then Clay added, "But Fiona and I reconnected when she went to Chicago for college, against Martin's wishes." And Clay had thrown that opportunity away by ignoring her and practically forcing her out of Chicago. He should have listened to her. She was his sister.

He turned off onto a narrow dirt driveway, not because he remembered it but because his navigation system told him to. He flipped on his headlights since the trees lining the driveway blocked out the light. The car jumped and rocked on the pitted surface.

"Well, this is definitely a remote location," Joslyn said.

"Bobby's a survival expert," Clay said. "It's why he doesn't have a phone or cable TV or utility lines. He considers this cabin 'luxury living' because he's used to roughing it in the wild for days on end."

"You mean he likes doing that kind of stuff?"

"He took Fiona and me on some of the worst and best camping trips." Clay navigated around a narrow turn where the road was lined with trees and juniper bushes. "I saw him take down a bear once without blinking an eye. If Martin wanted to keep Fiona safe, he'd send her to Bobby. He's the first person I thought of when I saw that ornament, because the shop where it came from is only a couple miles down the main road."

They rocked down the driveway for another quarter mile before entering a clearing, with trees rising around it like sentinels. There stood a rustic cabin with weathered boards, but the yard and roof were clear of branches and leaves, and the small front porch had been swept recently. Despite the spring weather, Tahoe was a little chilly and a thin curl of smoke was rising from the brick chimney. Beside the house was a detached garage with a set of closed double doors, all made out of the same weathered wood as the cabin.

Clay parked behind the garage and tried to peer in between the cracks in the doors, but it was too dark and he couldn't see if Bobby's truck was there. He made his way onto the porch and knocked on the heavy wooden door. "Fiona! Bobby! It's Clay!"

"Does he like you?" Joslyn asked him as she peered through the front window. A curtain covered it but there was a narrow crack between the panels.

"Bobby?" Clay remembered him as a crotchety

old man with a heavily weathered face. "Well…
he didn't seem to dislike us."

She gave him an exasperated look. "That's very
helpful."

"He might lie to me about Fiona being here just
because Martin asked him to," Clay said, "but
if Fiona knew I was here, she'd come out." He
hoped. Had he burned his bridges with her the
last time he saw her?

He pounded on the front door again. "Fiona!"

"Fiona! It's Joslyn!"

But there was no answer.

They walked around the house and saw Bobby's wellhead and generator. The generator was
cold, so he hadn't used it anytime recently. They
looked in the windows but it looked as though the
cabin was empty.

"They're not here," Clay said. There was an
empty thudding in his stomach. He'd been so sure
she'd be here.

"They wouldn't have gone to town or something like that?" Joslyn asked.

"Bobby wouldn't if he was alone, but if Fiona's
here, maybe he would have."

Joslyn shifted from foot to foot. "Should we
wait for them?"

Clay thought about it, then shook his head.
"I'm not sure Bobby didn't just take Fiona camping to keep her off the grid. If he did, we'll never
find them."

"I still have a hard time picturing Fiona camping," Joslyn said with a delicate shudder. "Us computer girls don't do well without electricity. And toilets."

Clay smiled. "Fiona wasn't too thrilled about it, but there are some views you can only get to by going backpacking, and they're..." He took a deep breath, remembering in particular one isolated mountain lake, the sky above him so blue it almost looked fake. "Magnificent. Fiona's artistic side liked that a lot."

"I guess I can believe that. So what do we do?"

"Let's leave a note. If he's only out for a little while, he'll get it and call us." Hopefully.

"But he doesn't have a phone."

"He goes to the pay phone at the grocery store down the highway."

They found an old receipt on the floorboard of the car and he wrote a note to Bobby, leaving his burner cell phone number as well as Joslyn's. He slid it under the front door and hoped Bobby would notice it.

"Let's check into a motel and follow leads from there," Clay said.

"How will we know if he's got the message or not?"

"We don't," Clay said. "But I don't think he's taken Fiona camping. The porch is too clean. He's been home recently."

They got in the car and Clay did a three-point

turn in the front yard, then headed back down the narrow driveway. It was late afternoon, but because of the mountains and the trees, the path was dark and he turned on the headlights again.

As they rounded a sharp turn, they suddenly saw headlights down the driveway from them, snaking through the trees. Clay's hopes rose. "That's got to be Bobby."

He stopped the car as the other one approached, preparing for the difficult task of backing up the driveway, but then something about the lights made him pause.

They were too near the ground. Bobby's headlights were high up because he drove a Ford pickup truck.

That wasn't Bobby.

Clay couldn't let them be trapped on this road. "Hang on!" He gunned the engine. He knew he needed to take the occupants of the car by surprise or else the driver might simply turn sideways to block the road. They could just be lost tourists, but he didn't want to take any chances.

He almost made it. There was a curve with a treeless section near the edge of the road. He jammed the car onto the turnoff to swerve around the oncoming sedan. If he could slip past them, they could try to lose them on the winding mountain roads.

As his headlights flashed through the trees,

he thought he saw a familiar figure hidden in the darkness.

The sedan skidded on the dirt, the loose ground making it too hard for the car to gain traction, but suddenly it hit a hard patch and twisted sharply, turning sideways on the road. The sedan rammed into the front corner of Clay's car, shoving them hard into a stand of trees.

"Duck!" Clay grabbed Joslyn and shoved them both to the floor as bullets shattered the windows.

ELEVEN

Joslyn was crammed under the dashboard, her head tucked into her knees, as the sound of the gunshots snapped through the woods, partially absorbed by the trees. The shatterproof glass of the windows held, but a few stray bits rained on her head. Clay had his arms around her, his body shielding her from most of the debris.

"It's two weapons against one," she whispered. "I'm not that good a shot."

"I think Bobby's out in the woods."

"How do you know?"

"The headlights reflected off something...I think it's him, anyway." They both flinched as pieces of the window fell into the car.

Clay suddenly reached across to the other side of the passenger seat and pulled the lever to angle the back of the chair. It dropped to not quite full horizontal. "Out the back door. Come on!"

Joslyn spread herself out on top of the stretched-out chair and pulled the door handle to swing the back door open. She saw that the trees the car had hit had blocked in her own door, and the back door only opened partway because it was hampered by a huge bush. She slithered out onto the ground, then scrambled out of the way as Clay followed her.

He shouted to the men, "What did you do with my sister? I know you have her!"

Joslyn gave him a wide-eyed look that silently asked him, *What are you doing?*

"I'm telling Bobby it's me," Clay whispered. "Get your weapon out. You're going to have to distract them."

She could do that. She got her firearm and flicked the safety off, then eased it on top of the trunk of the car for a stable firing surface and looked out.

The woods were dark, but the sky above was still light and she could make out the men also crouched behind their own car. She'd thought it was right next to theirs, but it must have bounced backward after the collision, twisting around slightly so that it faced the way it had come with a stretch of driveway between the two vehicles.

As soon as the men paused in their firing, she aimed a shot at the rear bumper, where Met was hiding, and then at the front hood, where she thought G was. They answered with more gunfire.

"Police?" she whispered to Clay. How close were the neighbors? Surely they'd hear the gunfire.

"Too far away to get here quickly," Clay said. "When you fire again, I'm going to sneak around the woods to try to get the drop on G."

"They'll see you."

"It's getting darker. I'll be careful." He pulled his jacket sleeve down to hide the bright white of his cast.

She shot several rounds into their windows, spidering the glass and hopefully obscuring any view they might have had. She felt rather than heard Clay move away through the woods.

She crouched behind the car, her heart pounding, intermittent gunfire ringing in her ears. She didn't want to hit Clay, but she also wanted the thugs focused on her and not on the woods around them. She took careful aim and hit the taillight close to where Met was standing, and then the ground next to where she saw the edge of his shoe.

Clay had moved faster than she expected. He'd somehow crossed the driveway and sneaked up on G's other side, stalking him through the trees. He was just about to tackle G when the man turned and saw him.

The two went down in a tangle of limbs and there was a flash of white from Clay's cast as his jacket sleeve was shoved up. Joslyn saw G's gun arc in the air and land somewhere in the bushes.

The two men got to their feet. G swung at Clay, but he staggered backward onto the driveway.

Met had moved from the rear of the car to the front, but Joslyn shot out the headlights to keep him pinned down so he wouldn't try to help his partner.

But Clay was too hampered by his broken arm. G's roundhouse connected with Clay's left shoulder, and he winced. G followed with a second jab to his upper arm, then a blow to Clay's right jaw as his arm dropped. Clay stumbled backward and fell to the dirt.

G jumped on Clay, squirming around until he could wrap his arms around his neck in a choke hold. He twisted Clay's body around until it gave Met a clear shot.

Joslyn's heart was in her throat. She had to help Clay. But how?

"Give it up, Joslyn," Met called. "Or Clay dies."

The sound of a shotgun priming cut through the air.

"Get off my property."

The voice was deep and rough, as if it belonged to someone who had been woken up from a deep sleep. While the man spoke with a slow drawl, he emerged from the darkness of the trees with a mean look his eyes and his shotgun aimed at G and Clay.

G twisted around slightly to see the newcomer. Met aimed his gun at the old man.

Joslyn shot her last round near Met's head, and he yelped and ducked back down. She slowly, quietly reached into the open back door of the car, searching for her bag, which contained her second magazine.

"I'm giving you to the count of three," the man said.

Joslyn switched out her clip and looked. Met's attention was focused on the man.

"You'll hit Clay," G said. His tone was arrogant.

"I couldn't care less if I hit him," the man said. "One."

Joslyn took a deep breath, then darted across the road and landed behind the back bumper of the men's car. She aimed her gun straight at the back of Met's head where he crouched near the left front tire. "Drop your gun or I'll shoot," she said.

Met froze.

"Two."

"Okay, all right." Met suddenly raised his hands.

"What?" G gave Met an incredulous look.

Joslyn couldn't quite see, but Met gave G a look that made him shut his mouth. His eyebrows rose, and he gave an almost infinitesimal nod. Then he suddenly released Clay, who collapsed, gasping, on the ground.

The man kept his shotgun trained on G as he made his way back to the car. Met got in on the driver's side.

Without lowering his shotgun, the old man yanked Clay to his feet, helping him stagger to the side of the road.

The sedan's tires threw up dirt for a second before it finally skidded back onto the driveway, then drove away.

Only then did the man lower his shotgun. "You dumb fool." He smacked Clay in the back of the head.

Clay winced. "Nice to see you, too, Bobby."

"Who was that?"

"We're not sure. They're trying to keep us from finding Fiona."

"We're looking for her, too," Joslyn said.

"She's not here, obviously," Bobby said with a fierce look in his dark eyes. "And you're not the only ones who came here looking for her."

It had scared Clay, leaving Joslyn alone behind the car like that. But he hadn't known how else he could try to take out one of the two men and give Bobby a chance to help them. But he'd worried about Joslyn the moment he'd gone to sneak through the underbrush. She had distracted him. He couldn't let that happen again. He had to distance himself emotionally from her. He had to stop touching her, stop giving her stupid blue weeds.

Easier said than done.

She drew him, like a light in a window, shining

through the night. He had the feeling that when he came into her warmth and light, he'd be home.

No, he had to stop thinking like that. He wasn't fit for any woman to get to know. Maybe, once he found Fiona and got to apologize to her, he'd start on that road to finding a better version of himself. But not now. Not with someone like Joslyn, who clearly bore emotional wounds from the past. She deserved someone better than a screwup like him.

Yeah, he kept telling himself that, and he kept ignoring his own good advice. It was because she inspired him. He could tell she'd been scared, but she'd mastered her fear enough to take careful aim with her gun and use her bullets strategically. He could only admire her for that.

The local police arrived seven minutes after the men left, which was sooner than Clay had expected. Apparently Bobby's neighbor a half mile away had happened to be outside in her garden, heard the gunshots and called 9-1-1.Clay had been expecting another fiasco like in Phoenix and Los Angeles, but he'd forgotten that there were still a lot of folks who hunted in these woods and so gunshots were not as rare an occurrence to the Tahoe police.

Joslyn immediately gave them Detective Carter's name as reference, and the officers went to their squad car to call in and get in touch with him. They took their statements and were gone within the hour, promising to search for the men's car in the Tahoe area.

"If those goons are smart, they'll already have switched cars," Clay said as the squad car disappeared down Bobby's driveway.

"You told the police that you're looking for Fiona and those men have been following you," Bobby said. "Come inside and tell me the full story."

The inside of the cabin was exactly as Clay had remembered it, with the same leather couch and recliner, the handmade wooden bookshelf stuffed with paperbacks, the woven Mexican rug on the wooden floor in front of the stone fireplace. Everything was scrupulously neat and free of dust, which was so at odds with the way Bobby had gotten completely filthy on their camping trips. Clay had cheerfully followed suit while Fiona gave herself a sponge bath every day.

Bobby set a metal coffeepot on the wood burning stove in the corner. "Start talking, boy."

The raspy voice made Clay feel as if he was a kid again. Bobby was no-nonsense like Martin, and yet he'd looked at Clay as if he saw him whereas Martin had seemed to look straight through him. Bobby seemed to understand Clay's active nature and while he never actually praised Clay, he always included him on camping trips.

Clay explained about the phone call and postcard they'd received from Fiona, and then the bomb in Fiona's Phoenix house. That made Bobby's brows lower over his eyes, although he said nothing.

Clay told him about being followed in Phoenix, then the bomb in Joslyn's apartment and the siege on the house in Los Angeles.

"How'd they find you in LA?" Bobby demanded.

"We think they followed us from the hospital," Joslyn said. "My friends drove partway to LA to help us watch for a tail, but…"

"I thought we must have just missed them, or they were that good, especially if they had a three-or four-car team," Clay said.

"You said there were only two guys at the house in LA," Bobby said.

"I thought maybe the other cars in a multiple car team left once they knew where we were." In Chicago, Clay had worked as one of the cars tailing someone, and there had been a few times he was dismissed once the target reached the location. "But even a four-car team would have been hard not to notice on these mountain roads, and yet they found us here."

"When we changed clothes, I checked everything for GPS trackers even though the items were all new," Joslyn said.

"Phones?" Bobby asked.

"Our burner phones have been with us at all times with Bluetooth and WiFi off," Joslyn said.

"And after the bomb at my place, we dumped the phones we had and got new ones. They couldn't have followed us to LA through our phones."

"Any other personal items?" Bobby said. "Hair clips, necklaces? Your gun holster?"

"I checked everything, including my holster, but that's also been on me the entire time," Joslyn said dryly.

Bobby surprised Clay by barking out a laugh. "I suppose you're right. The car?"

"Checked before we left LA," Clay said. "But if it was small…"

"Take my truck," Bobby grunted.

Joslyn opened her mouth, saw the expression on Bobby's face, then closed it.

"Thanks," Clay said.

"It might put you in danger," Joslyn said.

"Naw," Bobby said. "I'll drive it to the trailhead and leave it until you find Fiona."

"Who else has come here looking for Fiona?" Clay asked.

"Martin," Bobby said.

Clay was too surprised to speak for a moment. "We thought Martin would send Fiona to you."

"What for?"

"To keep her safe," Joslyn said.

A strange look came over Bobby's face, as if strong emotion gripped him but his face was made of stone and he couldn't express it. "Martin Crowley cares about two things—money and bloodline. In that order. We're close because I'm his cousin, and I'm also the cotrustee of our grandfather's estate. Fiona…"

"Is blood," Clay said. "But not as important as his money."

Bobby said nothing, but he looked grave.

"So the reason he's looking for her has something to do with money?" Joslyn said. "He said that?"

"No," Bobby said. "But I know him. I've known him all my life."

"What did he say? When did he come?" Clay asked.

"About two weeks ago. He didn't say much, just saw Fiona wasn't here, and left."

Bobby wasn't one to ask questions, either. What was Martin's business was Martin's business. He'd always been that way.

Joslyn's eyes narrowed thoughtfully. "Who was he with?"

Clay didn't know what that had to do with anything until Bobby said, "Nobody."

"No bodyguards?" Clay asked. "What about his driver?"

"Nope," Bobby said.

"Martin drove all the way here alone?" Martin never did that. He always had someone drive him so he could do work while he traveled, even if it was fifteen minutes in between stops. It was at least seven hours' driving time between Los Angeles and north Lake Tahoe.

"I never saw that before," Bobby admitted, "but I wasn't about to ask him. He wouldn't have told me if I did."

"He's looking for Fiona all by himself," Clay said. "He doesn't want his own people to know he's looking for her."

"Or he doesn't want them to know where she is, if he finds her," Joslyn said. "What's going on? Those two men didn't seem to be working with Martin, and he doesn't even trust his own employees."

"We still don't know how Fiona got mixed up in all that," Clay said. "We need to figure out who she's running from. And where she'd go."

Joslyn shook her head. "No."

"What do you mean?"

"We do need to figure those things out, but more importantly, we have to figure out how these men are tracking us."

"The car..."

"We borrowed it from a friend of a friend of a friend. Do you really think they managed to tag it?"

No, he didn't.

She continued, "If we don't lose those leeches, we can't go looking for Fiona. Because we'll just lead them right to her."

TWELVE

It was three hours back to Sonoma, and the entire time, Joslyn mentally reviewed everything they had with them, and everything they'd done, trying to figure out how these men could be right on their heels.

"It's got to be a multiple-car team tailing us," Clay said. He had to speak louder than normal because Bobby's truck had a massive engine that made its presence known.

"If that's true, they could have taken us out on the freeway. There's no one else out at this time of night." Joslyn gestured to the empty highway, where only a few pinpricks of light could be seen from the oncoming cars in the opposite lane, and the one set of taillights ahead of them. "How long do you think it took between the time we parked in Bobby's yard and when Met and G started up his driveway?"

"At least ten minutes. Maybe more."

"If it was a multiple-car team, they could have

gone up that driveway sooner and had the drop on us when we were walking around Bobby's cabin."

"But after the hospital, we changed out everything. Clothes, phones, car."

"Maybe they planted something on us after the hospital."

"They didn't come in contact with us until LA," Clay said.

Suddenly she remembered the look on Met's face as he glanced at her just before walking into the hospital elevator. He'd been on Clay's floor.

"Your cast," she whispered.

"Met didn't get into my hospital room."

"He didn't get in the room, but I wasn't there when the doctor and nurse put the cast on. They asked us all to leave."

"There's a GPS tracker in my cast? It would fit?" He looked at his arm again. "I don't even feel it. You'd think I would have noticed it when the nurse was casting me."

"We know these guys are financed. They could find a GPS tracker small enough with a good enough battery."

"We can just wait until the battery runs out, right?"

"It's probably only broadcasting the signal once every few minutes," Joslyn said. "The battery could last days. Weeks."

"You want to take off my cast?"

"I couldn't, but Shaun's wife is a nurse."

"Okay," he said. "Let's do it."

He was fearless. In fighting Met and G each time, he had the kind of courage she'd only read about. She began to wonder if perhaps he didn't frighten her, like Tomas had, so much as startle her. Everything he'd done had been to protect her.

No, everything he'd done had been to help someone who could help him find his sister. There had been moments he'd looked as though he was attracted to her, but he never went any further. He backed away, or she did. It was as if both of them knew that getting involved wasn't a good idea.

She had to remember that. She didn't want strength, or charm, or excitement. Maybe it would be best if she went looking for someone boring, unemotional.

Except she'd never been attracted to men like that. She'd been attracted to charismatic men like Tomas. To strong, charming men like Clay.

She just didn't trust herself anymore. Maybe she never would.

It was past midnight, but Joslyn took out her cell phone and, using her Bluetooth headset, called Liam. "I need a favor from your sister-in-law, Monica."

"Are you guys all right?" There was an edge of alarm in his voice.

"We're fine, we're fine." She should have realized he'd be worried when she asked for a nurse.

"I want to take off Clay's cast. I think maybe it's got a GPS tracker in it."

There was a thoughtful silence. "That's a big maybe. You might reinjure his arm."

"Everything we got after the hospital was new—including the cast. But the cast is the only thing we didn't check for a tracker."

"Okay," Liam said finally. "I'll call her. How far away are you?"

"About two hours."

He groaned. "She's going to kill me. Meet us at my dad's house."

"If there is a tracker, is that wise?"

"There'll be four O'Neills with shotguns. I think it'll be okay."

She hung up and told Clay, who frowned fiercely. "I don't like it."

"I can testify that the O'Neills can take care of themselves."

"I don't like not knowing the kind of house and how defensible it is."

She started listing the description, as she remembered it. "Two-story. Overhanging back deck on the second floor. Motion-sensing floodlights. About one-acre backyard, landscaped with flowers and bushes, a few trees."

Clay surprised her by laughing. In fact, he laughed so hard that he almost folded in half where he sat on the passenger side.

"What's so funny?" she demanded.

"Not funny. Ironic, I guess." He snickered again. "I would've liked working with someone like you in Chicago."

"Not sure that's a compliment."

"You're smart, observant, logical. Concise."

She wasn't sure how to respond to that. "Um… thanks," she said after an awkward silence.

"Doesn't anyone compliment you?" He looked offended for her.

When Tomas had complimented her, it was on her face, her body, her clothes, her smile. Later in the relationship, he'd complained that she was too geeky and analytical—he wanted her to be more "feminine."

The guys in her classes either saw her as competition, or one of the guys, or both. Liam and Elisabeth saw her as herself, but they were also protective because of what she'd been through last year.

Clay…he made her feel powerful. And confident. And beautiful.

"I'm just not very good at accepting them," she said.

"Sorry, did I embarrass you?"

She shook her head, and too late realized it looked as if she actually was embarrassed. Sometimes she was such a dork.

"You're such a geek." Tomas's lip curled as he studied her.

She shoved the memory away. She never had to see him again.

Clay reached all the way over with his right hand to touch her left wrist. "Don't rub your scar," he said.

As usual, Joslyn hadn't realized she was rubbing it.

But it was too late—the remembrance of Tomas had caused a chunk of ice to lodge itself in her chest. She was quiet for the rest of the drive.

When they got to Sonoma, she drove toward the O'Neill family home. Shaun and his wife, Monica, were living there and taking care of Shaun's father, Patrick, who'd just completed his last round of chemo treatments a few months ago. Liam's duplex rental had sustained damage last year and he'd moved into the family home while he saved up to buy some property and build a house.

Clay's frown grew fiercer as they drove up to the house and parked in front. "I don't like this."

"I heard you the first ten times you said that." Joslyn unbuckled her seatbelt and got out of the car.

"We're leading those men directly to Liam's family." Clay slammed the door a bit harder than necessary. "If they're like my guys were, they'll have gotten reinforcements this time."

"Shaun is former border patrol. Liam is ex-military. Patrick is a Vietnam War veteran. If Elisabeth is there, she has the best aim out of all of them. They're not exactly helpless." There were several cars parked in the large circular driveway, and she recognized the dark sedan. "And Liam called Detective Carter, too."

He looked grudgingly appeased. Joslyn thought she knew why he was being like this—he didn't like seeing others hurt. He didn't want to be the reason anyone got hurt.

And that reason might be embedded in his cast.

They were all in the living room sipping coffee, the three O'Neill men, Monica, Detective Carter and Elisabeth. And another man she didn't know. She could sense Clay tensing beside her, and she laid a gentle hand on his arm.

Monica came forward first, so Joslyn said, "Clay, this is Shaun's wife, Monica."

"Nice to meet you." She shook Clay's hand. "This is my cousin, Dr. Geoffrey Whelan," Monica introduced the stranger. "He works at my free children's clinic. I wasn't comfortable taking the cast off myself, so I called him."

Geoffrey had a calm, strong demeanor, and he shook their hands. Up close, she could see he had the slightly exotic features of someone half-Asian, just like his cousin, but Joslyn couldn't see much of a family resemblance.

"You're okay taking this off?" Clay half raised his cast.

There was a glint in Geoffrey's eye. Joslyn

realized that he knew Clay was testing him, challenging him. "According to Liam, you've been followed, attacked and shot at. If there's a GPS tracker in that thing, I have no problem taking it out."

"How do you take a cast off, anyway?" Joslyn asked.

"I brought some equipment from the clinic," Geoffrey said.

"Dealt with a lot of broken bones before?" Clay asked.

"I was in Japan when the tsunami hit and I was there for several years on medical missions. Trust me, I've seen everything."

That impressed Clay. He tilted his head, as if in acknowledgment.

"Clay, this is my father-in-law, Patrick." The man shook Clay's hand.

Then Patrick put his arm around Joslyn. "Hello, m'girl." He had almost adopted her like one of his own children since she'd come to Sonoma to work for his son. It had helped ease the loss of her own dad. "I see you're not staying out of trouble."

"You should talk," she teased him. "I heard you tried getting up on the roof last week."

"Completely exaggerated," he said.

Behind him, Monica shook her head violently and mouthed, *Not exaggerating*.

"Besides, I only wanted to watch Shaun, Liam

and Brady out on the lawn. They were doing that wrestling stuff," Patrick continued.

"You wanted to shoot the water cannon at us, Dad," Liam said dryly. "And it's not wrestling, it's mixed martial arts."

"Clay, here, is supposed to be pretty good." Shaun threw some mock jabs at Clay. "We'll wait until you're healed up. That way you can't claim it's your injury when we make you tap out."

Clay grinned. "Bring it."

Detective Carter yawned and exited the room, followed by Geoffrey, and Monica said, "Enough trash talking. Geoff's got to go to work in a few hours. Clay, why don't you—"

Suddenly, the darkness outside the windows lit up in a blaze of white light. They all froze for a second.

Shaun's brows drew low over his eyes. "The yard floodlights are motion-sensitive."

Then a gunshot cracked through the night.

There was a small spray of sparks, and one of the outside lights went out.

"Down! Everyone down!" shouted Detective Carter. He dragged Patrick onto the floor even as he pulled out his cell phone to call for backup.

Clay moved toward Joslyn and shoved her to the ground, half covering her with his body.

"Oof! What are you doing?" she hissed.

"Stay down." There were more bullets, and he

could hear thuds against the wood of the over-hanging deck.

"They're trying to take out the outdoor flood-lights attached to the deck," Shaun said.

"Gun cabinet," Patrick said as he crawled toward the far side of the living room. Liam and Shaun followed him, but Detective Carter crouched low and opened the glass door onto the second-story deck. He dropped to his belly and scooted to the edge, firing his gun out into the yard. "There's four of them!" he called back to them.

There was a tinkle of glass as another flood-light went out.

Clay wanted to roar with frustration. Because he'd been in prison, he wasn't allowed the use of a firearm. He looked around the room and spot-ted a massive orange handheld searchlight charg-ing in the corner.

He dived for it, unplugged it, then darted out to the deck, crawling on his stomach next to Detec-tive Carter. He turned on the light and a blazing white beam shone down onto the manicured lawn.

There was movement to his right, in the area darkened by a broken floodlight, and he swung the flashlight toward it. A man froze, temporar-ily blinded. It was one of the men from the BART platform, the one who had grabbed Joslyn.

"Police!" Detective Carter shouted. "Drop your weapon!"

The man raised his gun at the light, and Clay.

Detective Carter's gun rang out, and the man flinched and ducked behind a bush.

The detective grunted. "Missed," he muttered.

Suddenly Joslyn was next to him with another orange searchlight.

"What are you doing?" he hissed.

"I'm not a good shot with a rifle," she said calmly.

"Get back inside."

"No way." She flipped on the light and shone it down into the yard.

Another shot from the men in the yard hit one of the slats of the wooden railing around the deck. Joslyn, Clay and Detective Carter ducked as splinters rained on them.

"Get inside!" Clay roared at her.

"Shut up and cover the yard!" she yelled back.

She spotlighted another man who was trying to sneak into the house. It was G. As soon as he was exposed, he leaped away, looking for cover, except there wasn't any nearby. He raced back toward a row of planters.

Suddenly Clay noticed Patrick, Monica and Geoffrey all on their stomachs on the deck, aiming rifles out at the yard. "Get off my property!" Patrick yelled, and fired.

It seemed they weren't aiming to kill or injure, but the shots fired into the ground began herding the attackers back and away from the house.

The men were no match for three rifles and one handgun. Two of them suddenly raced away to the far end of the property, out of range of the searchlights.

"Hey!" one of the remaining men shouted to them, but they didn't pay attention. After a moment, that man turned and ran after them.

"The neighbor's access road is that way." Patrick pulled out his cell phone. "I'd better warn them."

"Tell them to stay in their house," Detective Carter added.

"I only see three of them," Clay said.

Detective Carter frowned. "There were four."

Suddenly, a wailing alarm pierced Clay's ears. It was followed by a second alarm, pitched slightly higher.

"That's the house alarm!" Patrick shouted. "And the fire alarm!"

Shots from high-caliber rifles came from the front of the house. Clay leaped to his feet and ran through the glass door into the living room. He started toward the front of the house and began to smell something different from the acrid gunpowder out on the deck. Smoke.

Clay suddenly understood. The attack on the back deck was a diversion.

The front room of the house was on fire.

THIRTEEN

Clay sat on the O'Neills' back lawn with everyone minus Detective Carter, who was coordinating with the police officers and firemen who had responded to his calls.

"We're lucky it's fire season," Liam said. "The fire truck got here pretty quick."

According to Liam and Shaun, who'd gone to the front of the house, one of the men had thrown something through one of the front windows, maybe a Molotov cocktail, which had splattered accelerant all over the front living room. The broken window had set off the house alarm, and the burning living room had set off the fire alarm.

Shaun and Liam had battled the blaze with fire extinguishers, but it wasn't enough. They'd given up and taken Clay with them out the back door. Everyone on the back deck had filed out down the outside stairs and onto the back lawn while Detective Carter had called the fire department.

The four men had taken off.

"I don't understand," Joslyn said. "Why attack us that way? They knew we were inside. They could have tried something more stealthy."

"I think the floodlights surprised them," Shaun said.

Clay nodded. "There was that pause between when the lights went on and that first shot."

"I think they didn't realize how far out the motion sensors were for the yard lights," Shaun said. He pointed to his left, where there was a ground sensor several hundred yards from the back of the house. "They expected to be able to get closer. When the lights went on, they tried to take them out."

"They wanted to smoke us out," Liam said. "Then they could take Clay and Joslyn."

"Too bad they didn't know who they were dealing with," Patrick said grimly.

"I hope there isn't too much damage," Joslyn said.

"It looks like they put the fire out quickly," Monica said.

"I needed new furniture anyway," Patrick said.

He'd need more than new furniture, Clay was certain. He'd probably need to remodel his front living room. "I'm sorry, sir," he said to Patrick.

The older man reached out and his large hand wrapped around the side of Clay's face. "It's not your fault, son. I just thank God that you were here to help us take out those scumbags." He smiled at Clay, and dropped his hand.

Clay sat there, unable to move. These people gave acceptance so freely. He hadn't had to earn it, the way he'd earned his place in the mob family or even the way he'd earned the respect of his sparring partners at his gym back in Illinois. These people made him feel that he belonged.

It almost made him believe that his past didn't matter.

But that was dumb. His past would always matter.

"Is that an electrical outlet?" Geoffrey pointed in the direction of the motion sensor.

"Yeah," Shaun said. "We have yard lights we put up out here to play flag football."

Geoffrey grabbed his medical bag, which he'd remembered to grab out of the living room before following them down the deck stairs. "Then we can take Clay's cast off."

"Now? Here?" Joslyn asked.

"You want to wait for them to attack again?" Clay said. "Let's do it." He'd brought the orange searchlight with him, and so he flicked it on and handed it to Joslyn to hold in place.

It was strange to be sitting on the grass, Monica holding his arm steady while Geoffrey plugged in something that looked like a power tool from his high school shop class.

"Isn't that just a regular saw?" Shaun asked. "I've got one of those in the garage."

Monica gave him a sour look and backhanded his shoulder.

Geoffrey, seeing Clay tense, gave him a small smile. "Don't worry, this is a cast saw. It won't cut through your skin." He turned it on and began working, making cuts on both sides of the cast. Then he got a metal tool from his bag and spread the cast pieces open, revealing padding and a stockinette underneath, before lifting the pieces away.

As Geoffrey cut through the softer layers around Clay's arm, Joslyn picked up one of the pieces and examined it in the light from the flashlight. Her jaw tightened and she pointed to a shadow in the cast. "There it is."

"I don't see it."

"Hand me the cast saw."

"No way," Geoffrey said without looking up. "I'll cut it out as soon as we recast his arm."

Monica wrapped a new cast on Clay's arm while Geoffrey used the saw to cut out a small electronic device, attached with a wire to another device like a flat button. "That's the battery, I think," Joslyn said.

"Cut the wire," Liam said to Geoffrey, who did so. "That'll keep it from transmitting."

Clay let out a low breath he wasn't aware he'd been holding. "We need to leave."

"You're not going anywhere, son," Patrick, said.

"But those men know we're with you," Clay said.

"The GPS is off, so they won't know if you're still with us or not," Liam said.

"How'd they even get that in there?" Elisabeth demanded.

"It must have been Met," Joslyn said. "Not him directly, but he was at the hospital. He must have bribed a nurse or something."

"Well, they gave him this plaster cast, which means it was only temporary," Geoffrey said. "He's probably scheduled to get a fiberglass one in a week or so. That man could have convinced the nurse that it was only a joke. She'd know the cast was coming off in a week, anyway."

Clay picked up the tiny device, with bits of plaster still stuck to it. He had to control himself to keep from crushing it in his fist. "I didn't even notice the nurse putting this in there."

"It was right over the padding," Geoffrey said. "It would have been easy to slip it in place before wrapping it."

"We should still get this to Detective Carter," Liam said. "He can look into the nurse who did it. She might have noticed something about Met or whoever asked her to do this."

They could use any information they could get, because really, what did they have? Bobby's cabin had been a bust. They had a box of books and junk that didn't give any clue about what caused Fiona to leave LA, much less why she was gone.

Clay got to his feet. He couldn't sit anymore, feeling useless with only one good arm and a bruised body. What had he done in the past few days besides putting Joslyn in danger? Besides putting her friends in danger?

Liam crossed the back lawn toward the house, intent on giving the tracker to Detective Carter. The sun was rising, coloring the horizon gold and pink, interrupted only by evergreen trees breaking the smooth rolling foothills. The light shone warm on the wood of the O'Neill home. From this angle, Clay couldn't see the gutted front room.

He shouldn't have stuck with Joslyn. Those men might not have cloned her phone if he hadn't been with her. They might only have gone after Clay, since he was Fiona's brother. She wouldn't have been shot at. Patrick O'Neill's house wouldn't have that massive fire damage. He was only lucky no one got hurt.

Lucky. He'd rarely been lucky in his life. His knee twinged, and he reached down to rub it.

"Mixed martial arts injury?" Patrick had come to stand beside him, both of them watching the house and the firemen and police officers swarming around it.

Clay shook his head. "Older. Not one I'm proud of."

"Oh?"

Clay didn't often share about his past, but he'd lain on Patrick's deck and the man had shot a rifle at intruders Clay had brought to his house. He figured he at least owed the man an answer to his idle curiosity. "Back when I worked for a Chicago mob family, I was chasing a guy who owed my boss money. I slipped on some wet stairs and tore my ACL and a mess of other tendons. I don't remember their names."

Patrick grunted, then tapped his right thigh. "Not quite the same, but I got a bullet in my kneecap in Nam. Never quite healed right."

Here was a veteran. Clay was just a low-level mob thug. Why was he here with them all? He didn't belong.

Patrick continued, "When a man can't walk, it changes your perspective on things."

Clay was about to give a noncommittal answer when he realized that for him, it was true. "It made me realize how little I meant to my bosses. I thought I had friends there, but I didn't, really. I had decided to try to leave the mob when they got busted by the FBI."

"Did you cut a deal?"

"I didn't have much the FBI wanted, so there wasn't much of a deal I could cut. I got two years. But when I got out, the mob family was defunct. I could move on."

"It's hard to walk away from your past," Patrick

said. "You try to fit in with the real world again, and you just don't belong."

Clay had never compared his time in prison with a war zone, but he supposed that coming out of both could be similar. And he didn't belong. Not with these people.

Then Patrick touched his head again, like he had before, as if Clay were his son. "I'm not telling you this to make you feel bad. I'm telling you this because I know that look at the back of your eyes. I felt it when I came home from the war. I saw it in Shaun's eyes when he quit the border patrol. It's still in Liam's eyes when he thinks about the explosion that got him sent home from the army. I'm telling you that with prayer, and the people around you who love you, it'll go away eventually."

Love. Who did he have who loved him? His mother was dead. He'd chased away the only person left, his sister. And he'd been trying to keep himself distant from Joslyn, because he somehow knew she was his Kryptonite.

"I know what you're thinking, son," Patrick said. "And you'll just have to forgive an old man for giving advice to a man he doesn't know very well. One of my favorite Bible verses is First Peter four, verse eight. 'Love covers over a multitude of sins.' You think on that."

Patrick left him to go back to where his son and daughter-in-law were sitting on the grass.

Geoffrey had leaned back and seemed to be asleep. Joslyn was talking to Elisabeth.

These people had love. They knew how to receive it and how to give it. Of course they'd feel content, self-assured.

No, Clay realized, Patrick wasn't talking about their love for each other. He'd quoted a Bible verse. Joslyn mentioned God every so often as if she really knew God, like they had a friendship and a bond.

Love covers over a multitude of sins. God's love?

But there was no way God could love someone like Clay.

He stood apart from them all, but he felt no desire to join them. And yet a part of him wanted to belong to them. A part of him was afraid to consider that maybe he'd been alone for most of his life, even when he was in the midst of his friends, his posse, his crowd. Maybe he was just meant to be that way.

He was getting morose. It was lack of sleep. When he found Fiona, everything would be better. He could apologize to her. He could make amends for not listening to her. He could reforge that relationship.

He could finally find redemption.

Joslyn felt a bit like Godzilla, leaving destruction in her wake. Fiona's house was bombed, so was her own apartment, and now Patrick no longer had a front living room.

Which was why she, Clay, Liam and Elisabeth were at Elisabeth's apartment, also known as the O'Neill Agency headquarters. Liam was saving up for a custom-built house which they would eventually use as their official office, complete with a top security system in place, but until then, Elisabeth's computers and servers were ranged all over her dining room, living room and one of the two bedrooms.

Joslyn checked one of the computers, nicknamed Leviathan, a particularly powerful custom-made desktop with the ability to run her facial-recognition program. She'd written the code with the help of Monica's cousin Jane Lawton, another computer programmer.

"Any matches?" Elisabeth asked.

"Not yet."

Liam frowned. "It's been running for over a day, now."

"It's crawling through the entire web, looking for a photo that might match the pictures of Met and G that we got," Joslyn said. "It's a marathon, not a sprint."

Liam threw up his hands in surrender, although he gave her a smile and a wink.

What was she doing, causing all these problems for her friends? She'd already gotten Liam and Elisabeth involved with her ex-boyfriend and a dangerous drug gang last year. Now she was battling some seriously financed thugs with high tech she would drool over if she weren't running for her life.

"Anything I can do?" Clay asked. He had his newly casted arm in a sling, but his entire body hummed with energy despite his lack of sleep the night before. They'd caught a couple hours, napping on the back lawn while the police finished up, then they'd come here to Elisabeth's apartment to do research. Clay hadn't wanted to leave Joslyn alone, even though he admitted he barely knew how to log in to his email.

"Can you cook?" Elisabeth asked.

He grinned. "I make a mean breakfast burrito."

"Then you're on food duty while we work."

He saluted her and headed to her kitchen.

Joslyn felt guilty for dragging Clay into this, but strangely, she had the feeling he took all this danger and uncertainty in stride. She didn't like not knowing, not being able to control anything. But for Clay, nothing seemed to faze him. He did what needed to be done. Period.

That was completely the opposite of how Tomas had been. He'd been emotional, easily upset, always stressed. At first it had made him seem very romantic and exuberant in his attention toward her, but then...

She managed to stop the memory before it found her. Her breath was even, her heartbeat slow and steady. She felt strong, in control. She felt like…Clay. He made her feel confident.

She hardly knew him, and yet she felt that he would be a good person to get to know. He would bring out a better side of her. He could help her heal.

She couldn't remember what that was like, to be healed. To be whole.

"Joslyn?" Elisabeth's soft voice invaded her thoughts. She realized she'd said her name a couple times.

"Sorry."

Elisabeth touched her shoulder and asked in a low voice, "Are you okay?"

She knew about the baby. She'd seen the most dramatic effects of Tomas when Joslyn had first run away. She'd seen her at her worst, and had helped her and cared for her.

Joslyn took her hand and held it for a moment. "I'm getting better." Her counselor had told her not to dissemble, to be honest but not a complainer. It had felt good to be able to say how she really felt with people who cared about her. It was like sharing a burden.

"Since Leviathan's running the facial-recognition program," Elisabeth said, nodding to the desktop she'd made herself, "go use the computer on the table."

"What about Liam?"

"He'll use the one in the bedroom. Just tell him what you want him to look for."

"Martin Crowley. Fiona. Anything she might have done in Los Angeles besides her school-work."

"Let's split it up so we don't overlap," Elisabeth said. "I'll dig into some of the government databases I have access to." She did some contract work for the FBI in San Francisco, which was why her computer systems were so strongly encrypted and protected. Joslyn had gotten some of her best security tips from Elisabeth.

"I'll take Martin, you take Fiona," Liam said to her.

They had started working, each at various computer stations around Elisabeth's apartment, when a sudden ping broke the sounds of clicking mouses and tapping keyboards. There was a surprised silence, then Joslyn launched herself at the Leviathan and looked at the screen.

Her web crawler program had found a match for both men, in the same photo. It was an article posted on the website for a small Los Angeles business magazine. At first, Joslyn thought the program had made a mistake, because the photo was a smiling shot of a businessman standing at an outdoor podium, addressing a crowd.

Then she looked behind the businessman. In the background, Met and G were standing there in an alert, yet relaxed stance. They looked like bodyguards.

"Who is this?" Joslyn scrolled through the article.

"Wait, stop." Elisabeth was reading over her shoulder. She pointed to the screen. "Richard Roman."

"What did you say?" Clay's tight voice shot out from the doorway to the kitchen. The too-small, bright yellow apron he wore contrasted sharply with the thunderous look on his face.

"You know him?" Liam had come out from the bedroom, where he'd been working. "Who is he?"

Clay shook his head in frustration. "I should have guessed. Martin almost ruined him, or something like that. Fiona told me about it when she was still living in our apartment in Chicago."

"About what year was that?" Elisabeth went to her computer, which was the most powerful out of all of them, and began typing.

Clay told her. It was the year before he'd gone to prison, so only a few years ago.

While Elisabeth searched, Joslyn looked up the basics on Richard Roman, and discovered something interesting. "Clay," she said, pointing to her computer screen. "Look where Roman's office building is."

"It's near Martin's."

"It's near that *candy shop*."

Clay blew out a breath. "We thought Met and G

were connected to Martin because of that Chinese candy Met was eating in that video, but maybe it's because they were connected to Roman, instead."

Elisabeth said, "I found the connection between Roman and Martin."

Joslyn read over Elisabeth's shoulder. This was a newspaper article in the *Los Angeles Times*, but it was just a small blurb about how the bidding for the sale of Balthazar Corporation had unexpectedly gone to Martin Crowley of Crowley Industries, when Richard Roman of RRC had been the expected winner.

"I don't understand," Joslyn said. "How did that ruin Roman?"

"Fiona said something about how Martin's bid was lower than Roman's, but they sold the company to Martin anyway," Clay said. "I'm afraid I didn't really understand what she was saying."

"How'd he get them to do that?" Elisabeth asked. "Bribery? Blackmail?"

"Whatever it was, the deal was stolen from Roman," Liam said.

"And he sent those two men," Clay said. "They rigged Fiona's house. And Joslyn's apartment."

"They've been trying to kill us," Joslyn said. "And maybe Fiona, too? But why?"

"Revenge," Clay said, his voice low and somber.

Joslyn felt a tightening in her chest. "He wants Fiona to get back at Martin. You remember what Bobby said—"

"Martin cares about money and bloodline," Clay said. "Fiona's his only child, as far as I know."

No wonder Fiona had disappeared. How had she known Roman was after her? "So would Roman hurt Fiona just to get back at Martin?" Joslyn thought about that. There was something that didn't quite fit in place. "That seems kind of emotional for a cold businessman like Roman."

"And Martin cares for her," Clay said. "He'd have hidden her away somewhere safe. Why didn't she go to him for help?"

"Wait, wait." Joslyn snapped her fingers. "Martin went to Bobby's cabin by himself, looking for Fiona. Without his secretary, his bodyguards, his driver. He didn't trust any of his people. He probably thought they'd sell Fiona out to Roman."

"I think they must have already sold her out to Roman," Clay said slowly.

"What do you mean?"

"When Martin saw Fiona in Phoenix at that museum, he had his guards with him. And then Fiona disappeared soon after that."

"You're right. Martin's people must have told Roman she was in Phoenix," Joslyn said. "So if Martin's people can't be trusted, Fiona wouldn't have anything to do with help Martin could give her."

"You're forgetting about the postcard," Liam said. "And the phone call."

"Were those from Fiona, or someone Roman hired?" Joslyn said. The implications of that weighed on her.

Clay's uncertain look told her he understood the same thing. "If we try to find Fiona, we might be leading Roman right to her."

"But can we really take a chance that the postcard and the phone call weren't from Fiona, and just do nothing?"

Clay scowled. "I can't stand by and do nothing when she might be in danger."

"With our help," Liam said, "you can shake anyone trying to tail you."

"Wait a minute," Elisabeth said. "This isn't just danger to us or to them. This is danger to Fiona, too. Remember last year? We didn't go looking for you because we didn't want to lead Tomas right to you."

Clay's eyes narrowed. "Who's Tomas?"

Joslyn swallowed and looked away. "My ex. He's in prison now."

Elisabeth gave her a silent look of apology as she realized Joslyn hadn't told Clay about Tomas. "If this is revenge, then there's a good chance that these men not only want to hurt Fiona, they want to make her suffer in order to make Martin suffer."

Joslyn pointed to Roman's face on the computer screen. "But what if Fiona's not safe and that's why she sent the postcard and called Clay?"

Joslyn met Clay's determined eyes, which were gray flint. "I don't feel right not doing anything, especially when it seems like Martin is frantically searching for her, too. We have to know she's okay." She had to know Fiona was alive.

Clay nodded. "This is the closest we've come in days. At least we now know what she's running from."

"So we can try to figure out where she would go," Joslyn said.

Elisabeth sighed. "All right, I understand. But you need to take precautions."

"That's what you and Liam are best at," Joslyn said.

Liam laughed. "Are you actually trying to charm us? You're finally learning, grasshopper."

"I didn't learn charm from you," Joslyn said. "I learned it from Clay."

Caught by three pairs of eyes, he froze, and a flush shot up his face. Joslyn had never seen a man blush so fast. Then his smile came out and he turned on that famous charm. "Aw, shucks, just 'cause I could convince a Hawaiian to buy sand…"

"Let's get to it," Liam said. "I'll work on your 'precautions.' You and Elisabeth try to figure out where Fiona would go to hide from Roman."

"There might be a connection between Roman and Fiona," Joslyn said. "I'm still not convinced that he's only after her for revenge."

Clay had that caged-tiger look on his face. He must hate not having much to do. "Breakfast is ready," he muttered, and turned to go back into the kitchen.

Then she realized… "You need to look through Fiona's box again."

He raised an eyebrow at her. "I do?"

"She's not just running from Roman, she's running from anything connected to Martin, because she's in danger from his people."

Comprehension dawned. "So she'd go somewhere Martin wouldn't know about."

Joslyn nodded. "You're the one who's known her the longest. Maybe Chicago? I thought the box might jog your memory."

He nodded and went to get the box, which they hadn't removed from the trunk. Joslyn got the breakfast burritos and passed them out so they could all eat and work at the same time. Clay set the box on the table while Joslyn and Elisabeth each sat at a computer and planned how they'd do research.

"She'd go somewhere Martin wouldn't know about," Joslyn said around a mouthful of eggs, cheese, and tortilla, "somewhere that a private investigator or a skip tracer wouldn't be able to find no matter how much they dig up on Martin."

"So let's track Fiona's movements for the past few years and compare them to Martin's movements," Elisabeth said. "And maybe cross-reference that with Roman's movements."

Joslyn groaned. That was a lot of data to find and compare.

"Wait a minute," Clay said. "I need you to look up something first."

Joslyn looked up at him.

He was holding up the Disneyland picture from Fiona's box. "I think I know where Fiona is."

FOURTEEN

Behind the wheel of their newly borrowed car, Clay was exhausted but fighting the tiredness. He had to stay alert for Fiona.

He'd grabbed a couple hours of sleep while Joslyn and Elisabeth searched for Amelia, Fiona's childhood friend. It took them longer than expected because Amelia had married and divorced, and her mother, Hannah, had died a few years earlier. While Clay originally chafed impatiently at the delay in going to see Fiona, as soon as he sat on the couch, he'd been out like a light while they worked.

Liam had borrowed yet another friend of a friend's car for them just in case Roman's men had noted their car in the O'Neills' driveway. Clay liked this one, an Impala that had once been black but was now mottled with various shades of gray, and with an engine that said, "Nobody messes with me."

"Um, despite the lack of a paint job, this is

a nice car. What if it gets bullet holes or something?" Clay had said nervously to Liam.

"Unless they injected a GPS tracker under your
skin, they haven't figured out how to follow you
yet," Liam had said. "And with this engine, hopefully you can speed away from guys with guns."

They were currently driving south on Interstate
5, with Liam and Elisabeth following them in two
different cars, watching for anyone tailing them.
But in central California, Liam and Elisabeth exited
the freeway, as preplanned, in order to turn back to
Sonoma. Clay and Joslyn were on their own again.

Joslyn was dead to the world, her mouth hanging open a little as she slept in the passenger seat.
He knew she needed the rest. They were both running on fumes right now.

But he couldn't sleep peacefully until they
found Fiona. They were close. He knew it.

Amelia rented a house in a small suburb north
of Los Angeles, quite a distance, in terms of com-
muting time, from the downtown areas. However, the suburb was quiet and the houses a bit
larger than in areas nearer to the city. Most of the
buildings were fifty or sixty years old, some better maintained than others. They stopped in front
of a beige house with blue trim that had, in the
middle of the front lawn, a Redwood tree so large
that the tips of its lower branches almost reached
the edges of the yard.

The tree overshadowed the front door and almost blocked the front glass window, but the shades were drawn anyway. Clay thought that was a little strange since it would make the inside of the house pretty dark.

They knocked, but no one answered. Joslyn knocked again, and Clay moved to the front window to try to peer inside through a crack in the curtain.

The front room was dark, but he could see that it had a small flat screen television against one wall and a large open space on the carpet in front of it, with a couch shoved against the opposite wall. Toys littered the carpet and an empty toy basket lay on its side, but it didn't look as if a child had been playing—it looked as if the basket had been tipped over, the toys thrown onto the floor in haste…or in a search.

Instantly he went on alert, his ears open to any sounds, his eyes scanning the exterior of the house, the neighbors, across the street. Everything was quiet except for the drone of an afternoon game show from the neighbor's television.

"What is it?" Joslyn's eyes were wide.

"Just a…feeling." He moved around to the side of the house and found another window. It was a bit higher up off the ground so he had to jump to get a look inside.

It was a bedroom. And it had been completely tossed.

His heart rate ramped up. He jumped to take

another look just to be sure. Yes, the dresser drawers were half-open, contents spilling out, clothes all over the bed, while closet doors were left open with hangers that had clothes only half hanging on them.

"Something's wrong," Clay said.

Joslyn had already unholstered her gun and held it at the ready. "Is the gate to the backyard open?"

He tried the wooden gate that separated the front from the backyard, and found that the latchkey was unlocked. The hinges creaked as he swung it open, and he froze, listening for any movement or sounds. Nothing.

He led the way into the backyard. He knew Joslyn had the firearm, but he wasn't about to let her step into any danger. He'd rather take any hits first.

The yard was open and sunny, with a large bushy lemon tree in the far corner and lavender bushes along the wooden fence. Plastic children's toys were scattered across the grass, and there was a concrete, unshaded patio that led to a sliding glass door. A black Weber grill stood on a corner of the concrete square, and there was a glass-and-metal patio set that took up most of the space. None of it was disturbed.

Clay moved silently toward the sliding glass door, which was obscured by vertical blinds that had been pulled closed. He peered through the cracks and saw that the kitchen table right next to the glass door also looked as if things were thrown on top of it and rifled through.

He noticed that the screen door inside the sliding glass door was cracked open. He grabbed the handle of the glass door and pulled.

It opened easily. Clay's fingers tightened on the handle as he froze, listening.

"Let me go in first," Joslyn whispered.

"No way."

"You've got a broken arm. I've got a firearm."

"No way." Clay stepped inside.

One or two drawers in the kitchen were half-open, and Clay wondered if someone had left in a hurry, as opposed to someone searching through the house. They moved from the kitchen to the hallway, which was also littered with toys, mostly from Disney. The first room on the left was a child's room, and it looked as messy as the bedroom he'd seen.

Joslyn moved past him toward the other doorway before he could hiss a warning. She eased open the door. "It looks like she packed quickly and took off."

"Does it look like it was more than one person?" Maybe she was helping Fiona.

Joslyn shook her head.

"She took her daughter with her." Clay nodded to the bedroom. "She only has one kid, right?"

"Yeah, why?"

"This seems like a lot of stuff for one kid."

Joslyn peeked into the room and chuckled. "Trust me, it's for one kid."

They searched through the house, but couldn't figure out where she could have gone. There were computer cables in the wall, but no computer. There were lots of pictures on the walls, mostly of Amelia and her daughter, and a few of Amelia with her mom, Hannah.

There were also several pictures with Amelia and a guy who might be her boyfriend. He had wavy brown hair, and in the majority of the photos, they were out hiking somewhere. They apparently liked Santa Cruz, because there were three different pictures of them hiking there.

"Boyfriend?" Clay asked.

Joslyn frowned. "I didn't find anything online about a boyfriend, but she's not very active on social media, so it's possible."

Joslyn then went to the fridge and started looking at everything stuck to it with magnets, most of them also from Disneyland.

"What are you looking for?" Clay asked.

"She's a single mother, so she has to have some type of card with phone numbers for babysitters," Joslyn said. "Yup, here." She pulled an index card from the side of the fridge that had Amelia's cell number, work number, and the name and number of her daughter's doctor.

Joslyn put the phone on speaker and tried Amelia's cell. It went straight to voice mail.

Then she tried Amelia's work number.

"Hello?" answered a gruff man.

"Is Amelia Richardson there?"

"She quit weeks ago." The man then hung up without another word.

Joslyn frowned, then dialed the baby's doctor's number.

A woman with a pleasant voice answered, "Hello, Ms. Richardson. What can I do for you?" The doctor's office must have caller ID.

"Hi, you know, I don't have my calendar in front of me. When's Jessica's next appointment?"

"Oh, you're not scheduled for another few months. September twelfth."

"Okay, thank you," Joslyn said, and hung up. "Well, she might still be in the area."

There was a number at the bottom of the card, written in a different pen color from the other numbers, which said Gabe.

She dialed the number, and it went straight to voice mail. "You've reached Gabe Speight with Speight Associates. Leave me a message and I'll get right back to you."

Clay had the phone book out before the message finished. He searched and found Gabriel Speight's address listed. "Think she went there?"

"If I were scared enough to quit my job? Yeah," Joslyn said. A haunted expression passed across her face briefly, as if she knew exactly what that felt like. His hand clenched at the thought of someone terrorizing her like that.

Joslyn moved away slightly.

Clay wanted to reach out to her, to hold her, to help erase that pain. But what did he know about healing people? For most of his adult life, he'd only hurt others. He'd protected a few people, like the women at the club he worked at, but he didn't know if that made up for all the ones he'd roughed up.

"Let's go," he said.

Instead of exiting through the back door, Clay locked it from the inside, and they exited through the side door, which could automatically lock behind them. As they were walking onto the front lawn, he noticed sound of the television from the neighbor's house had turned off and an older Asian woman was outside on her front lawn, watering the plants along the fence. The expression in her dark eyes was fierce. "Who're you?"

"I'm an old friend of Amelia's," Clay said.

"I've never seen you around before," the woman replied, still hostile.

"I haven't seen her or her mom, Hannah, since we were kids," Clay said. "Our moms had season passes and took us to Disneyland all the time when we were living in Los Angeles."

The neighbor relaxed a bit at that information. "She still goes to Disneyland all the time."

"Her back door was open, so we went inside, but we locked up behind us," Joslyn said. "Do you know where she is?"

The woman shook her head. "Hasn't been home in a few weeks." However, by her tight-lipped expression, she wasn't about to enlighten them on where Amelia might have gone.

"We were going to Gabe's house to see if she's there," Joslyn said. "Did you have any messages for her?"

The woman seemed to unwind a bit. "Well, tell her I borrowed her shovel from her tool shed."

"Will do." Joslyn and Clay waved goodbye to her and got into their car.

They looked at each other, and said together, "Gabe's."

Gabe lived farther south and closer to the downtown areas. His high-rise apartment building sat on a block with a coffee shop, a florist and another tall building that held law offices. They found street parking and walked to the glass-fronted building.

For some reason, Joslyn seemed tense as they walked through the front doors into the lobby. There was a security guard in a uniform sitting behind a large desk made of faux blond wood and a glossy black top. "Hi, folks," he said.

"We're here to see Gabe Speight," Clay said, leaning against the desk.

"Is he expecting you?"

"No, but tell him it's Clay Ashton." He hoped that if Amelia or Fiona heard his name, she'd know he wasn't here to hurt her.

The guard got on the phone and dialed. "I have a visitor for you, a Clay Ashton?"

The silence was tight. Clay feigned casual disinterest and confidence that they'd be allowed up, but it took all his self-control not to fidget. Would it work? Was Amelia or Fiona there?

"All right." The guard hung up. "Go right up."

Clay had to restrain from doing a victory fist-pump. "Thanks."

Joslyn started walking toward the elevators, then asked Clay, "What's the apartment number, again?"

"Er…" Clay looked back at the guard.

"Three-oh-two."

"Thanks."

As they rode the elevator, Clay's leg jiggled. Fiona had to be here. It was safer than her house, because of the security guard, but they'd still managed to finagle their way in. He had to get her somewhere even more secure.

They knocked on the apartment door, and a woman's voice inside said, "Who is it?"

"Amelia, it's Clay, Fiona's brother. Is she all right? Are you okay?"

There was the sound of the deadbolt sliding back, then the door cracked open. "Come in."

Something was wrong. Clay entered slowly,

eyes searching the apartment. Directly ahead of them were floor-to-ceiling windows along one wall, with a leather couch and small dining room table in front. A few Disney toys were scattered on the floor.

He and Joslyn entered the apartment, then there was the sound of a gun safety clicking off.

Clay turned and saw Amelia, standing to the side of the open door, holding a pistol to Joslyn's head.

Joslyn stood stock-still. Her blood roared in her ears, and all her senses were trained on the feel of metal caressing the skin of her temple.

Clay put his hands up. "Amelia, it's me. We're not here to hurt you."

"I haven't seen you in years. Why have you suddenly shown up? And here? How did you find me?"

"Please put the gun down first," Clay said. "We're looking for Fiona. I got a phone call from her three weeks ago. She said, 'Help me, Clay' and then got cut off. And Joslyn got a postcard from her with the same message."

There was a tense silence, then the muzzle of the gun dropped from Joslyn's head, and she heard the safety being clicked back on. She suddenly felt as if she could breathe again, and the air returned to her lungs in hard gasps.

"Is Fiona here?" Clay asked.

"She's not here," Amelia said, sounding weary.

Clay deflated visibly. He'd been so hoping for Fiona to be here. Joslyn had been hopeful but cautious, because she remembered how mindful Fiona was of others. Joslyn couldn't see Fiona holing up with Amelia and her daughter, putting them both at risk.

"How did you find me?" Amelia asked.

"We know Fiona is running from one of Martin's enemies," Clay said, "so we figured she'd run to someone not connected to Martin at all. You're the only friend Fiona had who Martin never met. He hated Disneyland, so he let Mom take me and Fiona alone."

A small smile quirked the corner of Amelia's mouth. "We had so much fun there." Then her eyes grew wide. "You weren't followed, were you?"

"No," Clay said. "And I'm pretty sure Martin doesn't even remember your friendship with Fiona from her childhood. We went to your house and found Gabe's address, so we came here."

"If Fiona isn't here, why did you run?" Joslyn asked.

"Because Fiona told me to."

Clay drew in a sharp breath. "You saw her."

Amelia nodded. "Three weeks ago."

"Can you tell us what happened?" Clay asked.

Joslyn heard voices outside the open door and ducked her head out to check. A man on his cell phone had just opened an apartment door with his key and was walking inside. She closed the front door to Gabe's apartment and locked it.

At that moment, there was a faint cry and a small fist pounding on a closed door in the apartment. "Mommy!"

Amelia hurried to the hallway and opened a bedroom door, picking up a little girl with Amelia's brown curly hair and button nose.

Joslyn smiled at her. "She looks just like you in that Disneyland picture."

"What picture?" Amelia asked.

Joslyn had tucked it, frame and all, into her bag and brought it out now. Amelia's brown eyes lit up at the sight. "I had forgotten all about that day. I got sick from too much ice cream."

"It's how we figured out where Fiona would go," Clay said.

"She came to my house," Amelia said, sitting on the couch with her daughter in her lap. "She was...frantic."

"Mommy, down," the little girl said, and Amelia let her play with some toys on the carpet.

"What happened?" Joslyn asked.

"She'd been kidnapped, but she escaped."

Joslyn couldn't speak for a moment. Clay had turned white. "Who kidnapped her?" he said.

Amelia shook her head. "Fiona said she didn't know. Two men grabbed her outside some museum. At a truck stop, she managed to get loose and hide, then she hitched a ride in the back of a farmer's truck to get away from them."

Clay gave a long breath. "She was okay?"

"She was fine, but scared. I told her to go to the police and she said she couldn't because of something with her father."

"When did she come to your house?" Joslyn asked.

Amelia told them the date.

"She came to you two days after Clay's phone call and the postal date of the postcard she sent to me," Joslyn said. "Why didn't she try to contact us again?"

"Did she mention anything to you about calling me?" Clay asked.

"No. She said she didn't want to put me and Jessica in danger, so she left after only a day or two. She told me to find somewhere safe, too, in case those men tracked her to my house."

Was that why Fiona hadn't reached out to Joslyn and Clay again, so that they wouldn't get involved? "She didn't tell you where she was going?" Clay asked.

"No, she purposefully didn't tell me," Amelia said.

Clay shook his head, his neck bent, a picture of defeat, but Joslyn wasn't done yet. She'd learned a few things from the way Elisabeth had managed to find out about Tomas and all the trouble Joslyn had been in last year in trying to escape him. They would find Fiona. They had to. "Amelia, what did you guys talk about while Fiona was here?"

"Well, a lot about Jessica." She smiled at her daughter, whose Disney princesses were having a heated discussion about who got to ride the stuffed unicorn. "She hadn't seen her in so long, she was amazed at how big she's gotten."

Joslyn sat up. Amelia's daughter was at least four years old, maybe five, but Amelia's comment meant Fiona had seen Jessica as a baby. "When was the last time you saw Fiona, before she showed up?"

"Oh, it's been a while...two years?"

"Two years?" Clay asked, surprised. "You and Fiona have kept in touch all these years?"

"You mean since we were kids? No, we lost touch when your mom moved to Chicago with you, because the only times Fiona and I ever really hung out was at Disneyland. But when Fiona moved back to LA, she called Mom and we got in touch again."

"Did you go to Disneyland with her?" Joslyn asked. "I went with her once." Fiona had gone to Disneyland maybe once or twice a year, and she usually went with her roommates, or whatever group of friends she could get together.

Amelia nodded. "I went with her once, too, but my marriage was falling apart at the time and my husband didn't like me going to Disneyland so much. Actually, when I divorced him, Fiona went with me and some friends on a trip to Hawaii."

"I think I remember that," Joslyn said. "It was just before Fiona left LA. She came back with a great tan. It was last-minute, wasn't it?"

"Yeah, one of my other friends had to cancel at the last minute, so I asked Fiona if she wanted to take her spot." Amelia frowned. "She was a little down on the trip."

"I remember she was a bit down just before she left," Joslyn said. "I never figured out why or what caused it."

"I talked to her about it a little, you know, when we were lying on the beach. It was two years ago, so I don't remember exactly, but I think she said something about being unhappy with her job."

"Job?" Joslyn shot a bewildered look at Clay, who looked equally perplexed. "I hadn't even realized she had a job." She'd seen Fiona almost every day for the months they'd been in the same master's program. They'd hung out, laughed together, had dinner and lunches together, and yet Fiona had never mentioned she had a job. "Did she say what her job was?"

"I don't think so. I don't remember it very well, so maybe she told me and I just forgot."

Maybe it was nothing. It might have been something she was doing for Martin and couldn't speak about because of a nondisclosure agreement. Was that why Fiona hadn't mentioned seeing Martin very often? Joslyn realized they still weren't completely certain if that was why Fiona had always bought candy from that store near Martin's office building.

"So what else did you guys talk about?" Joslyn asked.

Amelia thought a minute. "Gabe. We only started dating a few months ago."

"Did Fiona say she was seeing someone?"

"No." Amelia laughed. "She said the only romance in her life was from books."

Joslyn remembered all the romance paperbacks in the box she'd left at her old house.

"We talked about a lot of stupid stuff," Amelia said. "Our favorite restaurants, the latest thing trending on Facebook. Maybe we were avoiding the topic, or something like that. Honestly, I can't remember what else we talked about."

"What did Fiona have with her when she came? And what did she take with her?"

"Hardly anything. I let her take some of my clothes. She'd lost her phone, her jacket, and she said she pawned her watch in order to get out of Phoenix. I gave her a heavy jacket and a sweatshirt, and all the cash I had."

"How much?" Clay asked. "I can pay you back."

Amelia waved her hand. "Don't worry about it. She and I borrowed stuff from each other all the time…" She suddenly sat up straight. "Actually when I left my house, I put Jessica's stuff in a messenger bag that I borrowed from Fiona and kept forgetting to give back to her. It had some stuff inside she'd left there. Did you want to see it?"

Joslyn nodded eagerly, and Amelia went to the bedroom and returned with a large black over-the-shoulder bag made of heavy canvas. It had scuff marks and wear spots on the corners.

Inside, Joslyn found a little fairy doll, which she gave back to Amelia, and a romance paperback. There were also a few receipts for water bottles from kiosks in the Los Angeles airport.

"These aren't yours?" Joslyn asked Amelia, who shook her head. "Looks like Fiona used this for traveling." Had she taken this with her on those mysterious trips her roommates had mentioned?

Suddenly the door swung open and a man with wavy brown hair entered the apartment, carrying a briefcase. He froze at the sight of Clay and Joslyn, then shouted, "Who are you? And what are you doing in my apartment?"

FIFTEEN

Once he got over his anger and shock, Gabe was a great host. Clay couldn't blame him for being upset at seeing two strangers with his girlfriend and her young daughter, especially since Amelia had told him everything that had happened with Fiona.

Gabe had even cooked dinner for them, talking with them about safe topics like sports and the trips he and Amelia had taken, mostly hiking at various national parks in California, and showing them pictures. Amelia talked about what she had been up to over the past several years.

It was past midnight now, and Amelia was sleeping in one of the bedrooms with Jessica. Gabe had offered his bed to one of them, but they'd both refused. Clay had opted for some blankets and a pillow on the floor, while Joslyn took the couch.

Except neither of them were sleeping. They both sat at the dining room table, the lamp overhead the only light in the quiet apartment. Outside the glass windows, the many lights of Los Angeles sparkled.

They'd been brainstorming where Fiona might have gone, somewhere without a connection to Martin, somewhere remote. Clay had racked his brains and come up with a few ideas in Chicago, but a part of him didn't think Fiona would go back there.

"Did Fiona go to Sonoma with you?" he asked Joslyn.

"No, I never went to Sonoma until after she left." Joslyn sighed, then drew the messenger bag toward her. She pulled out the book and the receipts. "Would she leave the country?"

"She didn't have her passport with her when she was taken and she didn't want to go back and get it."

Joslyn suddenly squinted at the receipt in her hand. "This one isn't from the airport." She passed it to Clay.

It was a receipt from somewhere called Bara Grocery Store for a bottle of water and lemon drops. "Fiona likes lemon drops if she can't get Chinese candy," Clay said.

"Look at the totals."

Clay choked. "Fifty bucks for a bottle of water?"

"Is it really dollars? I didn't see a denomination." Joslyn reached for Amelia's laptop, which she was letting them borrow, and got online. "What's the address on it?"

"There's just a street number and name—1765 Ishibashi Street."

Joslyn typed, and suddenly turned the laptop so Clay could see. "It's not in the US. It's in the Tankoushoku Islands."

"I don't even know where that is." He stared at the online map she'd brought up, and saw that it was somewhere called Bara Island, in the Tankoushoku Islands, southwest of Hawaii.

Joslyn grabbed the paperback book. "This was in this bag. I wonder if she bought it in Bara, too." She flipped the book over and pointed to the price sticker. "Look, it's in Tanko dollars."

Clay looked over her shoulder as she looked up Bara Island. What they discovered blew his mind.

Joslyn's eyes were wide. "Bara is known primarily for offshore banking."

"Maybe she went on vacation," Clay said. "It's an island—maybe it has nice beaches, too."

"There's got to be a way to find out," Joslyn said, as if to herself. "Where's the box Fiona left at her old house?"

They'd kept the box with them and brought it in from the car. Clay put it on the table, and immediately picked up the shell. "See? Nice beaches."

Joslyn grabbed all the books, flipping them over to expose the price label. "These three are in Tanko currency."

"She could have bought them all at once."

Joslyn pointed to the date on the receipt. "Two of these books were published after the date on this receipt. She couldn't have bought them when she bought this stuff. She's gone back to Bara Island at least once more."

Clay picked up on of the books. "Fiona would use whatever paper she could find for bookmarks." He thumbed through the book and found nothing, but in the next book he picked up, there was a second receipt, again from Bara Grocery, for a different date. This receipt had both water and the book listed.

"At least three times," Joslyn breathed. "I can't think of any other reason she'd go here three times except for offshore banking accounts."

"But she's a software engineer, not an accountant."

Joslyn shook her head. "She took a few accounting classes."

Clay sat back in his chair. "Offshore banking. It has to have been for Martin." And Clay couldn't imagine his stepfather squirreling money away like this unless it wasn't legally obtained. "I can't believe Fiona would get involved in something like this."

"This might be why Roman wants Fiona," Joslyn said. "I always thought revenge was a strange motive for someone like him. But what if he wants to know about Martin's offshore accounts?"

Clay could suddenly understand how frightened and hopeless Fiona must have been. She couldn't contact Martin, because that was probably how Roman had found her in the first place, and she had nowhere to turn.

"This changes everything," Clay said. "It's not just revenge, it's money."

"It's why those guys were so persistent when they came after us," Joslyn said. "Roman's on a time clock. Once Martin realized Fiona was missing, he'd have taken steps to move his money. Roman can't use Fiona if there's no money in the Bara accounts."

"Is it only Bara? Maybe she knows other accounts, too. I wasn't directly involved, but I knew some of the accountants who worked for the Chicago mob family. When they needed to move money, it wasn't a quick process, especially if they had to set up other accounts to move it to. And they needed to move the money quietly, most of the time, so no one would be able to track it."

"So would Fiona lie low until Martin moved his money?"

"That would be my guess," Clay said. "Somewhere off the grid, isolated."

"Somewhere without a lot of people around," Joslyn said. "I know you said she didn't like camping with Bobby, but if she had to, she could, right?"

Clay winced. "Yeah, but I don't know that she'd

go survivalist. She'd try to find someplace a little more comfortable…" A picture flashed in front of his eyes of Gabe and Amelia hiking. "Of course! Can you check to see if Gabe or his family owns some type of cabin or vacation home somewhere? He and Amelia went hiking at Santa Cruz, didn't they? They had to stay somewhere."

Joslyn typed rapidly on the laptop, and Clay held his breath. If he were Fiona, that's what he'd think to do—look for some cabin, somewhere without too many neighbors around to ask questions.

Joslyn suddenly grinned, her smile bright as sunlight. "You're right. Gabe's family owns a cabin in the Santa Cruz Mountains."

"Someone just tried to run Liam off the road," Elisabeth said when Joslyn answered her cell phone.

"What?" Joslyn's hands jerked on the steering wheel and she adjusted her Bluetooth headset in her ear.

"What happened?" Clay grabbed the dashboard. His forearm was knots of corded muscle.

"He's okay," Elisabeth said. "He didn't get the license-plate number, but it was near downtown Sonoma, so Detective Carter is looking at the traffic cameras."

"Who was it?"

"He thought it was that guy you said was called

G. He only saw that picture of him once, so he couldn't be completely sure."

"Why Liam's car?" Joslyn asked, but then realized the answer herself. "Because we were riding in it, when we got back to Sonoma."

"The good news is that it means Met and G don't know where you two are or what car you're driving. And there are any number of friends of friends whose cars we could have borrowed."

"But Liam..." The last thing Joslyn wanted was for her friends to be hurt. And yet, look what had happened to Patrick's house, to her neighbors at her apartment complex.

"He's fine," Elisabeth said firmly. "It's not the first time he's had to employ defensive driving." The two of them had been on the run from not one but two Filipino gangs last year, and all on account of Joslyn.

The guilt gnawed at her. She was a walking disaster zone. This had to stop. They had to find Fiona, and protect her, and figure out how to stop Roman for good.

"Where are you now?" Elisabeth asked.

"We're on Highway 17, about to hit the summit," Joslyn said. "The GPS unit doesn't have a map for the mountain roads where Gabe's family cabin is, so we'll have to look for street signs."

"Those mountain roads are a maze. Be careful."

After Joslyn hung up with Elisabeth, she told Clay what had happened.

Clay's jaw muscles flexed. "Maybe we shouldn't have asked for their help. It's only brought trouble on your bosses."

"I was thinking that, too, but we couldn't have gotten so close to finding Fiona without their assistance."

Clay's expression grew pensive. "I have a hard time accepting people's help."

"I do, too," she said softly. "For a long time, it was just Dad and me. Finances were tough. It seemed like everything was a struggle. And the one time it seemed too good to be true, well, it was." Tomas and his charm, and the trouble she got into, dating a murderous gang captain.

He glanced at her, but he didn't pry, didn't ask her to explain. It was as if he shared her pain without knowing what it was, and she was grateful to him for it, because it was still too raw for her to be able to talk about it.

"It was just Mom and me, too, once she divorced Martin," Clay said. "He saw Fiona every weekend until he got full custody, but me…" Bitterness was ground into his words. "I wasn't his blood. He said he didn't want to see me."

She remembered what Bobby had said about Martin, and she suddenly realized how viciously, carelessly, he had cut into Clay as a boy, and as a young man, with his words and actions.

"I guess Martin taught me that you can't really trust anybody," Clay said.

She reached out and touched his shoulder briefly, softly. He gave her a smile that was like a flower opening up to the sun.

Was that what Tomas had taught her, too? To not trust anyone? But she'd trusted Liam, and Elisabeth, and the O'Neills.

Yet she'd also been trying to get back control of her life after the chaos last year. She never wanted to feel weak, afraid or vulnerable ever again. But had the experience made her be more guarded, more aloof?

And was that really the way she always wanted to be? She wasn't sure. It was safer, but was it good for her?

They turned off of the highway onto a road, which soon split into smaller roads that wound around the mountain. The woods on either side were sometimes sparse, sometimes thick, and smaller driveways appeared on either side almost like rabbit holes. Sometimes Joslyn caught a glimpse through the trees of a clearing and a house. The neighbors weren't quite as far away from each other as the homes in Tahoe, but there was enough distance and trees in-between to give a definite air of privacy.

It was also dark, because of the trees blocking out the midday sun and the mountainsides around which the road curved. But even more than that, the silence made Joslyn feel as if they'd entered an entirely different world. This was not like the suburbs or cities she was used to. This wasn't even the open rolling foothills of Sonoma that she'd lived in for the past six months. It was almost like a ghost town, except for the occasional wisp of smoke from a fireplace chimney that could be seen through the trees.

"How are we going to find the cabin?" she asked. "I don't see house numbers."

Clay shook his head. "We're wasting time looking for the house this way. There was that little grocery store on the side of the road right when we turned off of the highway. Let's turn around and ask directions."

Joslyn did a three-point turn in a driveway. As she did, she caught sight of a curtain twitching over the front window of the house at the end of the driveway, but other than that, there was no other sign of life.

Barnes Groceries looked like a long, rambling shack from the front, but was larger than it appeared once they went inside. There weren't many people in the store, and they found two employees chatting over the fruit they were setting out.

"We're hoping you can help us find our friend's house," Clay said.

The red-haired man who turned to Clay had a polite smile but a strangely wary expression in his eyes. "Oh?"

"Gabe Speight's family cabin? My sister's there, and we're trying to meet up with her."

"The Speight cabin?" The man's face grew strangely still, and he hesitated before answering. "Sure, that's not too far."

"Could you please draw us a map?" Joslyn asked. "I'm afraid we've tried to find it and got lost."

"Sure, sure." The man led the way to one of the cashiers and got out a pad and pencil. He drew a map, with a square for the grocery store and an X for the cabin. "Be sure to stay right at the forks. Otherwise you'll really get lost."

The man's words were friendly enough, but there was something about his demeanor, or maybe it was the placid expression on his face, which made Joslyn's suspicions rise.

"Thanks, we appreciate it." Clay said. He smiled at the man, but she noticed that the smile wasn't quite the same as when he had spoken to other people. There was a tightness about his jawline that made her think that his instincts were saying the same thing—something was wrong.

They got into the car. "I didn't get a good vibe from him," Clay said.

"Neither did I." Joslyn looked at the hand-drawn map. "So do we follow the map or not?"

Clay sighed. "Do we have a choice?"

"What if we're walking into something bad?"

"We've been in bad spots before. And Fiona might be out there. I have to at least try to protect her from Richard Roman."

As Joslyn started the car, she realized she would want Clay to pursue her this persistently if she were in trouble. She realized that after all they'd been through for the past few days, she trusted him to come for her if she were in danger.

She wanted to be that important to him.

She shook the thought away. Fiona was important now. And Clay was not someone she could invite into her life beyond these few days. She couldn't control him. She couldn't control or predict what would happen when she was with him, and that frightened her as much as a showdown with Met and G.

The map was detailed enough that they were able to follow it easily. They had driven only half of a mile, but the roads were so narrow that it took them quite a while. They were in the middle of a long stretch of road when suddenly a RAV4 came toward them, headlights beaming. It slowed, but strangely, instead of stopping a distance from them, it came almost up to their front bumper.

"Joslyn." Clay's voice was tight. He was looking behind them.

A pickup truck had pulled up. She hadn't noticed it because its headlights were off, and it also came right up to her rear bumper.

They were penned in.

Her heart rate shot up. She looked at Clay, who looked grim. "Now what?" she asked.

"Wait for them," he said. "It's their territory."

Two men got out of the truck behind them, while a woman and a man in a red ball cap exited the SUV in front. Joslyn felt rather than saw Clay tense when the man casually fingered a shotgun. Behind them, two more men came out of the pickup truck, also with shotguns.

The woman came up to the driver's side, a false smile on her face, and knocked on the window. Joslyn lowered it only partway.

"Mind stepping out of the car?" she said pleasantly.

Joslyn looked at Clay, who gave a tight nod.

She wasn't sure what she expected, but no one threw her against the car or threatened her. The woman stepped back a few steps to let her exit the vehicle.

"We aren't too fond of strangers asking about other people's houses," the woman said.

The man at the grocery store must have called these people and told them they were coming. Had he deliberately sent them this way to trap them?

"My sister is there," Clay said through gritted teeth.

"If she is, she'd have given you directions to the house," the woman said reasonably.

"Her name is Fiona Crowley and we think she's staying at the Speights' cabin."

"There's no one by that name in this area," the

woman said firmly. "Now I'd like you to turn around and be on your way."

"I just want to find her and make sure she's safe."

"If someone here needs protecting, we can take care of it."

"There is a man after her who will walk over dead bodies to find her," Joslyn said.

The two men behind them shifted nervously.

"He's been after us," Clay said. "We're trying to find Fiona so we can move her somewhere safe."

"How do we know you're telling the truth?" one of the men said.

"Shut up," the woman snapped at him.

Fiona was here. If she weren't, the man wouldn't have said that. "Please," Joslyn said, "just ask her if she'll see us. He's her half brother, Clay Ashton. I'm Joslyn Dimalanta and I was in school with her."

"She's not here," the woman said again.

"Ellen," one of the men hissed, "we're just bringing trouble on everyone by helping that girl."

"Shut *up*," Ellen said to him.

"You just like her because she fixed your wireless internet," the man shot back.

"She's been more neighborly than you have, Gordon," Ellen snapped. Then she stopped, and sighed.

"Please," Joslyn said again.

"Before I do anything," Ellen said, "you're going to hand me that gun in your flashbang holster, missy."

Joslyn was impressed she'd seen it, considering her shirt wasn't form-fitting. She turned her back to the men, reached in, and slowly drew it out, handing it to Ellen.

The woman nodded to the man in the red ball cap who'd been riding with her in the SUV. He turned and trotted back the way they'd come, and about fifty yards down the road, he turned off into a driveway almost hidden in the brush.

"Is Fiona there?" Clay asked. His body strained forward as if he could see through the trees.

"She's nowhere near here," the woman said. Joslyn had suspected that—if the red-headed man at the grocery store had warned these people, he had also mostly likely sent them down roads away from the house were Fiona was staying.

"She called me," Clay said. "Three weeks ago. I've been searching for her ever since."

"If she wanted to see you, don't you think she'd have called you again?" Ellen said.

"We know she's here so none of her friends and family would get hurt," Joslyn said. "But we found out who's after her and why. With her help, we might be able to stop him, and she'll never have to worry about him again."

Ellen considered the information. "You really think so, don't you?"

"I know what it's like to be hunted," Joslyn said.

Something passed across the woman's eyes, and there was a subtle change in her expression. "I believe you do," she murmured.

"You've only known her for three weeks, and yet you're protecting her like this."

"There's some who'd be happy chasing her off, because they don't want any trouble," Ellen said with a side look at the man who'd objected, "but most of us aren't like that. We take care of our neighbors—you have to, out here. And some of us know what it means to want to hide away."

A look passed between Joslyn and Ellen, and she somehow knew she'd earned a measure of respect from this tough mountain woman.

The man in the ball cap came running back up the road. "She said she'll see them."

Ellen nodded. "Gordon will drive your car back to the grocery store, and you two can ride with us."

"Are you sure about this?" said the ball-cap man. "How do we know they're who they say they are?"

"Use your eyes," Ellen said to him, glancing at Clay. Then she opened the SUV back door. "Clay, you're in back. Joslyn, you're up front with me."

They drove through winding roads, and Joslyn was almost positive Ellen drove in a few circles to confuse them. Almost twenty minutes later, they turned onto a long side driveway that had six houses ranged along it, three on each side, each with elaborate vegetable and flower gardens in front.

They stopped at the middle house, a two-story building with cream-colored siding and emerald green trim. The front door was on the side of the house at the top of a short flight of stairs, under a mini porch. As Joslyn got out of the car, the door opened.

And there she was.

This was the first time she'd seen brother and sister together, and she was again struck by how alike they were. Fiona's features were more delicate, but they had the same blue-gray eyes, the same blond-streaked, brown hair. Hers was pulled back into a ponytail. Until this moment, Joslyn had never realized how Fiona's intent expression mirrored Clay's exactly.

The siblings froze, staring at each other. Then Fiona burst into tears, running down the stairs and into her brother's arms.

SIXTEEN

Clay held his sister as tightly as he could with one arm, feeling her crying against his shoulder. He'd forgotten how small she was, how slender and fragile.

"It's okay, Fi." He stroked her back like he'd done when they were younger. His throat tightened even as his heart felt filled to bursting. They'd found her. And he'd never chase her away again. He'd protect her from Roman and anyone else who would dare try to hurt her.

When Fiona's tears had run themselves out, Ellen came up to them. "I'm assuming you're okay with these two, but did you want one of us to stay with you?"

"No, thanks, Ellen," Fiona said, wiping her face.

"Well, if you need me, I'm just a holler away." She gave Joslyn her gun and headed to the house next door to Fiona's, the first house on the lane. The other cars began to leave.

"Oh," Ellen called to Joslyn, "when you need your car, just come on over and we'll take you to the grocery store." Then she disappeared into her house.

"Hi, Joslyn." Fiona gave her a hug, too. "Come on inside."

Clay hadn't really noticed the cooler air here in the mountains until he walked into the house and felt the comforting warmth from the wood-burning stove in the corner of the spacious living room. There was also the scent of the cinnamon–orange-peel tea that Fiona liked.

Fiona grabbed some tissues from a box on the coffee table and blew her nose. "How did you guys find me? I was so sure I picked somewhere obscure."

"You did," Joslyn said. "We're just tenacious."

Fiona's eyes widened. "You didn't tell Dad, did you?"

"No, don't worry," Clay said. "We guessed someone in Martin's employ told Roman where you were."

"Roman? You mean Richard Roman? That's who's after me?"

"You didn't know?" Joslyn asked.

Fiona shook her head. "Have a seat. I'll get us some tea."

Clay made a face, and Fiona suddenly laughed. "You still hate tea?"

"I hate your herbal stuff. I want something bitter and caffeinated."

"You haven't changed a bit." Fiona headed into the kitchen.

Joslyn sat on the couch, and Clay sat next to her, taking her hand. "Thank you," he said. "This means more to me than just protecting her from Roman. I hadn't realized how much I missed her in my life."

She squeezed his hand, and her joy for him washed over him. "I'm glad you got this second chance with her. You can make up for lost time."

"I'm not going to waste it. If anything, I've learned that life's too short to not take risks. I want to take every moment I can to be happy with her."

Joslyn looked slightly startled at his words, but she squeezed his hand one more and then withdrew it.

Fiona came in with three steaming mugs, which she put on the table. Fiona shoved a mug toward him. "Bitter and caffeinated."

He grinned and took it. Then he reached out to take her hand. "You're okay, right?"

She nodded, looking down.

"Those guys who kidnapped you didn't hurt you, did they?"

"How did you… Oh, you probably talked to Amelia. That's how you found me, right?"

"You didn't make it easy for us," Clay said.

"It wasn't meant to be easy. Two guys had kidnapped me, after all."

"What happened?" Joslyn asked.

"I was in Phoenix. You guys found out I was living there for the past year or so?"

Clay nodded. "I hired a PI."

"I am a PI," Joslyn said. "Of sorts."

"I went to the local art museum. It's my favorite, so I'd been going often. And then Dad showed up one day, wanting to talk to me. I guess he found me the same way you did, although I really tried to hide my trail."

"Why didn't you tell him where you went when you left LA?" Clay asked.

"I didn't want him to find me." Fiona took a deep breath. "When I was in LA, I was helping Dad launder money and move it into offshore accounts."

They'd been suspecting something like this, but hearing his sister say it still seemed unbelievable. "Why? How? Did he force you?"

Fiona bit her lip and shook her head. "One of the reasons I left Chicago was because Dad had offered me a job in LA. He said it would have short hours and wouldn't interfere with my degree program. But what he really wanted was my computer expertise to help him launder his money and move it into his accounts in Bara."

There were tears in Fiona's eyes as she looked up at him. "I was so ashamed of what I was doing for him, Clay, after all the grief I gave you over your mob connections. And there I was doing illegal things for my own father. I was mad at you when I left Chicago, but I had always intended to call you and reach out again…except I couldn't."

"Hey, it's okay." He moved to sit next to her, even though it was squished in the loveseat she sat in, and put his arm around her. "You know, if prison taught me anything, it's that we all make mistakes."

"At first I was kind of excited about how much money I was making," Fiona said. "But then I started to hate it more and more. Finally I left LA because I couldn't keep working for Dad, and I just wanted a clean break. I thought I'd managed to hide from him, but he found me at the museum and said he'd known all along where I was."

"What did he want?" Clay asked.

"Apparently he'd found out that some of his accountants were skimming, so he moved a bigger chunk of his money into his Bara accounts and changed the passwords. He wanted me to come back to work for him because he knew he could trust me and no one else knew about those accounts."

"Someone did, or Roman wouldn't have tried to take you," Clay said.

"I don't know how they'd have found out. No one except Dad knew I was in charge of the Bara accounts. Dad paid all my travel expenses himself in cash, not through the company or any track-able lines of credit."

"Roman's got some sort of mole in Martin's company. He's been trying to find you himself, without any of his people around him. We think it's because he doesn't trust any of them."

"I wondered about that," Fiona said. "I told Dad I wouldn't work for him again and I left the mu-seum, but then two guys grabbed me in the park-ing lot. The thing is, I know Dad's driver saw me, but he deliberately turned away. That's when I knew it had to do with Dad somehow."

No wonder Martin had decided to ditch his em-ployees to search for Fiona alone.

"They didn't know I had my phone in my pocket," Fiona said. "I was wearing cargo pants and they missed one of the pockets near my knee when they searched me. They put me in the back seat of their car and drove for a while, but then they stopped for gas. I went to the bathroom and tried calling you, Joslyn, but both your numbers were disconnected."

"I lost both numbers last year," Joslyn said.

"So then I called you," Fiona said to him, "but they realized something was up, because they broke into the bathroom and took my phone."

"What about the postcard?"

"I managed to steal one of those prestamped postcards when they were dragging me back out to the car," Fiona said. "I found a pen in the back seat of the car and scribbled that note as fast as I could. Then at the next gas station, I put it in the mail slot. But I managed to run away from those guys and hide—the gas station was right next to a big truck stop. And then I snuck onto the back of a farm truck to get away. I sold my watch to get a bus ticket to Amelia's house."

Clay gave her a one-armed hug and felt her body trembling from recounting her story.

"Is Amelia all right?" Fiona asked.

"She's fine," Clay said. "She's staying with her boyfriend."

"I didn't want to stay with her for too long because I didn't want to put her in danger, but it gave me the idea to go to Gabe's family's cabin to hide out. I figured it would make it harder for anyone to find me."

"We didn't put it together until Gabe talked about the hiking trips he and Amelia go on all the time."

"I know." Fiona made a face. "Ew. Hiking."

Clay and Joslyn laughed. It felt good to have something like that to laugh about after the danger and chaos of the past few days.

"So you went to Amelia because you didn't trust your father's people?" Joslyn asked.

"Yes. But I didn't know who wanted me kidnapped or why and the men who took me didn't offer any clues."

"We've had two guys after us for the past few

days, because we came to Phoenix looking for you," Clay said.

"Oh, no." Fiona's hand tightened in his.

"Hey, we're okay."

"Oh, yeah." She poked at his cast. "Sure. You're great."

It probably wasn't the best time to talk about the bomb at her house and at Joslyn's apartment. Clay cleared his throat. "Anyway, we got a photo of them and Joslyn has some spider web program—"

"It's a web-crawler," Joslyn said. "A friend and I have been working on a facial-recognition program that looks for photos on the web."

"Whoa," Fiona said. "You need serious processing power for that. Did you—"

Clay cleared his throat. "Remember, Neanderthal in the room."

"I'll tell you later," Joslyn said to Fiona with a smile.

"The two guys work for Roman," Clay said. "You seem to know him?"

"I've heard of him. Before I started working for Dad, they were rivals. But then Dad outsmarted him in some business deal and Richard Roman was livid."

"We think that one of the reasons he wants you is because of your knowledge of the offshore accounts in Bara," Joslyn said.

Fiona's brows furrowed. "But it's been three

weeks. Dad must have contacted his private banker to arrange to transfer the Bara money to some other account by now."

"I don't know if Martin knew you were gone right away, especially if one of his people arranged for Roman's men to take you," Joslyn said thoughtfully. "We went to Bobby's house in Tahoe, and he said Martin came around looking for you only two weeks ago. Perhaps the money hasn't been moved yet."

Fiona thought about it. "Maybe not. He might still be in the process of transferring it. Once he does, the accounts I know will become obsolete."

"He might still come after you," Clay growled. "You know about Martin's finances and contacts, and Roman might want to target you just out of revenge against Martin."

Fiona gave a short, hard laugh. "Like Dad would care."

"What do you mean?" Clay asked.

"Dad doesn't care about me," Fiona spat out. "Do you know what he said when he saw me at the museum? It was all about his money, and how his accountants had betrayed him. He knew I'd never betray him because I was his blood and so I'd feel the same way about his money."

"He cares about you because you're his blood," Joslyn said.

"He was like that even when I was working for him in LA. He was never interested in me, or my friends, or anything in my life. It was all him and his business and the work I was doing for him. It's another reason I wanted to leave and not tell him where I was going."

Fiona looked at Clay. "I was always so sorry for how he treated you when he and Mom divorced, for how he just didn't seem to care. I made excuses for him because it seemed like he loved me. But he didn't—he was grooming me to work for him, or maybe eventually take over his business, I don't know. He only cares about himself, and I'm sorry I never saw that." Her arms tightened around him, and tears fell down her cheeks. "I'm so sorry for all the arguments we had back in Chicago. I was so hypocritical. I was too ashamed to contact you again."

"Hey, it's okay." He squeezed her tight, resting his head against her hair. "No matter what you've done, Fi, I will always love you."

"You have to," she said in a muffled voice. "You're my brother."

"I will always love you, too," Joslyn said. "I'll be here for you."

"We've spent three weeks looking for you," Clay said. "That's got to prove it to you."

"But with everything I've done," Fiona said. "I feel so awful."

"Love covers over a multitude of sins." He said it automatically, without even thinking, and he remembered it was Patrick's favorite Bible verse.

And he suddenly understood. It summed up how he felt about his sister—the things she had done didn't change the way he felt about her. So then, wouldn't God feel the same way about Clay and his past?

The O'Neills had accepted him, Joslyn had put her trust in him. Maybe he wasn't as worthless and unlovable as he'd always thought he was. As Martin had made him think he was.

Maybe he wasn't as alone as he always felt.

"So what happens now?" Fiona asked in a small voice.

"We find out how to stop Roman from coming after you," Joslyn said.

Fiona shuddered. "The past three weeks have been awful, looking over my shoulder all the time."

Joslyn nodded gravely. "I understand."

Clay wanted to know the story behind the empathy in her words. He wanted to protect her.

He also wanted to protect Fiona. He wasn't going to lose her again. There had to be a way to eliminate the threat against her and keep her safe.

But how?

SEVENTEEN

"I'm sorry," Fiona said. "I don't have any additional information on Richard Roman."

Joslyn realized that for some reason, she'd been hoping that once they found Fiona, suddenly all the answers to their dilemma would appear. Perhaps exhaustion was clouding her judgment.

"Then we need to take you to Sonoma to protect you," Clay said.

"No." Fiona shook her head violently. "I left Amelia because I didn't want to get anyone else involved in this. I even tried to keep aloof from the neighbors here, but they were so friendly, and then they needed help with their computers…" Fiona shrugged helplessly. "I don't want to put anyone else in danger."

"The O'Neills aren't just anyone," Clay said. "They can handle themselves and anyone else Roman throws at them. And it doesn't hurt that they're friends with a local detective."

"Your friends here can handle themselves, too,"

Joslyn said, "but my bosses are trained for stuff like this."

"Why can't I just hide out here until Dad has moved his money?"

"Like I said, the problem is that Roman might still target you even after the money is gone, if only to get revenge on Martin," Clay said.

"I'm not sure it'll make a difference to Dad," Fiona said bitterly.

"It'll make a difference to me," Clay told her fiercely. He wasn't angry—he loved her. He didn't want anyone to hurt her.

Tomas...Tomas had hurt Joslyn himself.

It was such a contrast, these two strong men, one an ugly memory who still seemed to have her in a choke hold as she walked through her daily life, and the other who had burst into her life like a whirlwind, who made her laugh, made her feel brave, made her feel safe.

"I just can't be comfortable until you're out of danger," Clay told Fiona.

Fiona sighed. "I know that, but if Roman is going to come after me no matter what, then what do we do?"

Joslyn sighed and admitted, "We don't have a game plan other than hiding you with my friends. We were hoping you'd have some information on Roman."

"How about we have lunch," Fiona said. "I'm

starving and even if I'm coming with you two, I'm not going on an empty stomach."

While Fiona made quesadillas for them, Joslyn called Liam and Elisabeth.

"We found Fiona," she said.

"Praise God," Elisabeth said. "So she's at Gabe's family cabin in Santa Cruz? That's pretty smart of her."

"But she didn't even know Roman was the one after her."

Elisabeth sighed. "Well, Liam and I have been researching Roman since you were on the road. I'll email you what we have."

"Thanks."

They sat down to lunch, and Clay was so obviously happy to be with his sister again that it nearly made Joslyn ache for him. He wanted to know what she'd been doing, all the little details of her life. Whenever she asked him about his life in Illinois, he shook his head and said, "I want to hear about you, first." It occurred to her that this was who he was, enthusiastic about life, loyal, giving.

Finally they finished lunch and they had to discuss what would happen next.

"I think it would be safer to take you to Sonoma," Clay said to Fiona. "Even if we don't know yet what we'll do, at least you'll have people around you who know how to protect you."

"These people know how to protect me," Fiona

said. "And you said yourself that Roman's men are in Sonoma. How will that be any safer?"

"She has a point," Joslyn said. Then something else occurred to her. "Hiding might spur Roman on, too, like a treasure hunt. Some men are like that."

Fiona said, "So if I can't hide, then what?"

"We need to make it so that if Roman so much as touches you, it would cause terrible repercussions for him," Clay said. "Something so bad for him that it would be enough of a deterrent to keep him away."

"I've been reading what Elisabeth dug up on Roman," Joslyn said. She'd gotten onto the WiFi in the house and logged in to her email to get the report. "One thing that stood out is that apparently Roman's company is not doing as well as Martin's. Actually, his company has been hemorrhaging money ever since Martin stole that bid from him."

"So taking Martin's money isn't just revenge, it's a need," Clay said.

"That would make sense," Joslyn said. "What if this is a long game?"

"A big con?" Fiona asked.

"Think about it," Joslyn said. "Roman found out about the Bara accounts somehow, and that you were handling them. He decides to manipulate the situation so that Martin would move more money into those accounts. All he'd have to do is get the other accountants to start skimming, and then get caught—maybe he bribed them, or blackmailed them, or maybe he made sure Martin found out about the skimming by leaking the information. Martin would naturally move his money into the only account that wasn't being mismanaged."

"That's exactly what Dad told me he did," Fiona said. "That's why he wanted me to come back to work for him, because so much of his money is in Bara Bank and he trusted me."

"Roman would really go through all that trouble, wait this long?" Clay asked.

"From what I've read about Roman, that's something he might do," Joslyn said. "Revenge is a dish best served cold, right?"

"So what do we do?"

The million-dollar question. They were silent as they thought about it, then Joslyn said, "What if we take away Martin's money?"

Fiona and Clay looked at her.

"We move the money from the Bara accounts?" Clay asked.

"No, not legally," Joslyn said. "And no, not move it from Bara. We make it inaccessible to both Martin and Roman in one fell swoop." She gave Fiona a hesitant look. "What if you testified against Martin to the FBI?"

Fiona was stunned, but Clay immediately picked up on what Joslyn was saying.

"Fi, you can cut a deal with the FBI," he said. "You get immunity, and you tell the FBI about Martin's money laundering. If the FBI arrests him, they can freeze all his assets."

"There would be no money for Roman to steal," Joslyn said, "not without a lot of high-tech work, and if he had those kinds of resources, he'd have already stolen the money from the Bara accounts."

"Roman would back off so he isn't singed by the legal heat on Martin," Clay said. "I've seen it happen before, although from the criminal's point of view. The authorities take out a criminal's victim or target—sometimes deliberately, sometimes accidentally—and so the criminal slinks away."

"It'll give the FBI—or us—time to find more information on Roman so we can put him away for good," Joslyn said.

"It's up to you, Fi," Clay said gently to her. "Whatever you decide, you know I'll be here for you."

Fiona chewed on her bottom lip. "It seems terrible to think about testifying against my own father." She looked up at Clay. "But I know exactly how he treated you. I know how he views me— I'm just a tool for him to use. That's the kind of person he is. He wouldn't hesitate to turn against me if it served his interests. I'll do it."

"You're sure?" Clay took her hand.

"I'm sure," she said. "But what about Roman after all this is done?"

"Let's worry about Roman after you're safe."

"We can ask Elisabeth to talk to her FBI contacts," Joslyn said. "The problem is that we're in a time crunch. Martin is moving his money."

"We have to act now," Clay said urgently. "Trust me on this. If he moves the money, it'll make Fiona's information on the Bara accounts useless to the Feds, and they'll have nothing to put a case together against Martin."

"How would he move it?" Joslyn asked.

"There's an underground banker he uses. Frank Devereaux. He's just outside of LA in a pretty remote spot," Fiona said.

"How can we get him to postpone the transfer?" Joslyn asked.

"You can't," Fiona said, her face turning pale. "But I can."

"No way," Clay said immediately.

"Maybe we can hack into his computers," Joslyn said.

"You'd still need to get close enough to do it," Fiona said. "He has surveillance cameras. He would spook if he saw anyone within a hundred yards of his property. In fact, he'd spook even if a camera went out."

"Continuous loop?" Joslyn said.

"We'd still need to get close enough to hack the camera feed. Look, he knows me. In fact...he's met both of you, too."

"When?" Clay asked.

"In Chicago. It was just before I left. Do you remember picking me up from school so we could go to the ballgame? There was a man I was talking to while I waited, and I introduced you. I said he was trying to recruit me for a job."

Clay's brows knit. "Yeah, I think I remember. Old guy, gray hair, kinda grouchy?"

Fiona smiled. "That's him. Martin had sent him to talk to me to see if I had the computer skills to handle the money laundering and his Bara accounts. At that time, Martin was using Frank for several accounts, but it was taking too much of his time to run them all."

"So Frank knows I'm your brother," Clay said.

"He also knows about your mob connections and the fact you went to prison, which might make him less suspicious about seeing you again."

"But I don't remember meeting anyone like that," Joslyn said.

"I didn't introduce you," Fiona said. "You walked me to the restaurant where I was meeting Dad for dinner because it was on the way to Mariella's apartment. Frank was outside the restaurant talking to my father. He left after I'd gotten there, but he saw you when you waved goodbye."

"He's not going to remember me from that."

"Before he left, he asked who you were. I told him and said you were the best hacker I knew. He said it was a pity my dad didn't need any more computer experts."

"Where are you going with this?" Clay said.

"Don't you see? The two of you could come with me."

Clay looked hopeful. Joslyn was wary, but at the same time, she knew what she had to do in order to protect Fiona. Still, she had to mention, "Do you think we should wait and let the FBI take care of this?"

Clay thought a moment. "The problem is that we're on a deadline. If Martin moves his money and we don't know where it went, it's Fiona's word against Martin's. There's nothing to prove she's telling the truth, and the FBI needs proof."

"Also, it's only been about two weeks," Fiona said. "If we go now and we find out the money's already been transferred, there's a better chance we can find out where Frank sent it before he erases the info from his computers. If we wait another day or two, it might be gone."

"Did you ever go see Frank with other people?" Clay asked.

Fiona bit her lip. "Usually only with a bodyguard."

"Then that settles it. Joslyn's not going."

"I am not staying behind," Joslyn said.

"I think we could use Joslyn's help," Fiona said. "Remember what I said about hacking his computers? It's not impossible, if we can get close enough. If Joslyn's there, either one of us can try to hack Frank's computers. If he's already moved

Dad's money, we might be able to find out where it's gone. If he hasn't, we'll be able to slow the transfer."

Clay looked mutinous, but Fiona folded her arms as if to make her point.

Finally he sighed. "All right, if you think this will finally get rid of this threat..."

"It will," Fiona said. "It has to."

"We can be there in a few hours."

"Joslyn and I need to create the hack, first," Fiona said. "Just a simple virus, I think, will do the trick."

Fiona happened to have a virus that someone else had created, which she'd found and saved, and so they worked to reprogram it to slow the money transfer. Fiona was most familiar with Frank's computer system, so she did most of the heavy lifting. It only took a couple hours, and Joslyn was glad that Clay took the time to sleep on the couch.

While Fiona was finishing up the hack, Joslyn went outside. The mountain air was cleaner, smelling strongly of fir and faintly of leaf mold. All was quiet, and above her, clouds skidded across the azure sky.

She dialed Elisabeth. She'd avoided telling her their plans because Elisabeth would want her to wait for the FBI to step in, but Joslyn didn't want to risk Fiona's life that way. They needed Martin's money in order to stop Richard Roman.

Joslyn was almost relieved when she got Elisabeth's voice mail. She left a message detailing what they were going to do, included Frank's location, then disconnected the call.

She smelled cedar and lemon zest and his deep, soothing musk just before she heard him come up behind her. Without turning around, she asked him, "Are we making a mistake?"

"Would you have been able to wait around, hoping the FBI would act in time, willing to put Fiona's safety in other people's hands, when you could do something about this whole situation right now?"

"It's just that it's so risky."

"Sometimes you have to take risks." Then, as if to put action to his words, he moved to stand in front of her. He cupped her face in his hands and bent to kiss her.

His kiss was like walking in a forest, the wind in her hair, sunlight on her face. The world spinning around her, full of possibilities, excitement, adventure. He was the kind of strength who would help her to be strong, to be able to believe even harder in a strong, sovereign God.

When he lifted his head, his hands caressed her cheeks. His eyes had darkened to deep blue like a tropical sea, and she felt she could drown in them.

Then he grinned, that irrepressible grin that never failed to lift her spirits. He suddenly bent down and picked a flower from the manicured flower beds lining the walkway leading up to the front door.

"Don't pick their flowers," she said weakly.

He handed her a bachelor's button, the same flower he'd picked for her outside the car rental office.

"What's this for?" she asked.

"A promise." He tucked it into her hair, like he'd done before. "We'll talk later about taking risks."

He turned and walked back inside.

Joslyn wanted that talk. But she couldn't suppress a shiver of foreboding that the risks they were taking now would turn their plans upside down.

It was full dark by the time they arrived at Frank's farmhouse, miles north of Los Angeles. The gleam from the car headlights reflected off the thick, waist-high weeds on each side of the country road, gold-and brown-colored from the dry season. The noise of the weeds swishing in the faint breeze put Clay's teeth on edge, because it made it hard for him to hear danger coming.

Fiona was pale, but only someone who knew her would notice. Her face was set in an uncompromising line.

"Won't Frank be worried if you're looking so upset?" Joslyn asked.

"I've never gone to Frank's place without being

upset," Fiona said. "He's incredibly annoying and I hated driving all the way here to deal with him."

They had parked next to the bent and battered mailbox that looked as if it had rusted open. There was no driveway.

Fiona walked along the road, shining a flashlight they'd taken from the car, then finally stopped in front of a scratched mile marker. "Here." She plunged through the weeds.

Clay let Joslyn go first, so he could bring up the rear. The path through the weeds was barely visible, even in the beam of his own flashlight.

"Don't stray from the path," Fiona told them. "Frank set land mines in the field."

Ahead of him, Joslyn started in surprise, then continued on. "Paranoid, much?" she muttered.

"He can see us on surveillance cameras, too," Fiona added.

Joslyn sighed. "Of course he can."

Her feisty spirit cheered him. He didn't want her to be here—he didn't want Fiona to be here, either—but he was glad he could protect them, even as injured as he was. He could still punch with his right arm, and there were some grappling moves he could do with a gimpy left arm. Fiona had said Frank wouldn't suspect him, so he wasn't going to let her out of his sight.

He wasn't going to fail her again.

The large shadow in front of them materialized into a two-story barn, made of a mix of wooden boards and metal siding. Motion-sensing flood-lights came on, glaring down at them. Fiona went up to the front double doors and pounded with her fist. "Frank!" She then stepped back and looked straight into a camera placed above and to the side of the doors.

There was a long moment of silence. Fiona frowned, and pounded on the door again. "Frank!"

An intercom buzzed and an annoyed man's voice said, "F-Fiona? What are you doing here?"

"Trying to save my hide," she snapped. "Let me in, Frank."

There was another long stretch of silence, where Clay counted his heartbeats. This was taking too long. He was about to say something when he heard the click of heavy locks being dis-engaged from inside the door.

Fiona froze. She looked back at Clay and Jos-lyn, her eyes wide but her mouth barely moving as she said, "He didn't ask who you two were."

Clay looked up at the camera. If he was as par-anoid as Fiona had indicated, why had he just let them in? He nodded for Fiona to go ahead and open the door, and he kept his posture deceptively casual, but his senses were on alert as he followed her and Joslyn inside.

Fiona pretended not to notice Frank's unchar-acteristic behavior. She stalked into the barn, past rows of metal shelving filled with electronic equipment, toward a bright light shining near the back. "Frank!"

"I—I'm here." A portly man with low, dark brows suddenly appeared ahead of her, standing in front of a long table filled with computers. "F-fiona, where have you been?"

There was the barest hesitation before Fiona answered, and Clay could tell by the tilt of her head that she had been surprised by something, maybe something he said, or maybe the nervous way he rubbed his fingertips together on each hand.

"I've spent three weeks hiding from the two thugs who kidnapped me," Fiona said, sounding annoyed. "It wasn't until yesterday that I figured out it was Richard Roman after me."

She walked toward him as she spoke, with Joslyn and Clay bringing up the rear. The barn was large and open with its concrete floor and high, bare walls. Everything told him something was wrong, but he knew they weren't followed here. So what was it?

Fiona went up to Frank and stood with her hands on her hips. "Listen, Frank, we have to move Dad's money from the Bara accounts. If they're empty, then Roman has no use for me."

"Oh, I'll think of something," said an unseen man in a smooth, confident voice.

Clay rushed forward to insert himself between Fiona and the source of the voice on their left.

In a swivel chair in front of a computer, legs crossed, hands steepled casually in front of him, sat Richard Roman.

EIGHTEEN

If Clay were a dog, Joslyn was certain he'd have been growling, hackles standing on end. He stood in front of Fiona and Joslyn and his attention seemed to be completely on Roman, but Joslyn was sure he was aware of a slight movement among the shadowy metal shelving just out of reach of the lights over Frank's computer desk.

"You must be Clay," Roman said with a smile that belonged in a boardroom. "If it weren't for the PI you hired, I would never have known you were even looking for Fiona. I certainly wouldn't have known about Joslyn, here. So thanks for that."

Met moved out from behind a piece of shelving, and he actually had his hands in his pockets and was snickering. G followed him, looking more serious with his body loose and ready, like a boxer about to head into the ring.

"Pity that bomb didn't kill you both," Roman said. "I'm sure you know Met and G by now, right? They've been trying to eliminate you for the past few days. I have to admit, you really did give them the slip when you figured out about that GPS tracker in your cast. I've got two other men scouring Sonoma looking for you two."

Roman's cold, dark eyes passed to Fiona. "You don't know Met and G, Fiona, but you'd know their associates. You spent a few hours with them."

"They weren't very good if they let a girl get away from them," Joslyn said.

"Very true." Despite his light tone, Roman twitched his shoulders beneath his expensive gray business suit, so Joslyn knew she'd struck a nerve. "They've been looking for her ever since—well, except for the side-detour to try to stop the two of you."

"Like I said," Joslyn said, "not very good."

"I'm not as trusting as they are," Roman said. "You can lose the gun in your flashbang holster, Joslyn."

She clenched her jaw.

"Slowly," Roman added. "You can hand it to Met."

Joslyn reached under her shirt to remove the gun from the front bra holster and glared at Met as she gave it to him.

Met grinned. "Maybe I need to search you."

This time, Clay really did growl, and the look

he shot Met could have melted iron. Met's smile hardened and he met Clay's gaze in challenge.

"You dogs can fight it out later." Roman sounded bored. "Joslyn, lift your pant legs, too."

She pulled each leg up, to show she didn't have a secondary weapon on her ankle.

"I doubt Clay has any weapons, but G, search him anyway," Roman said.

Clay looked ready to punch G when he made a move toward him, but Met simply raised Joslyn's gun and pointed it at Fiona. Clay stiffened but didn't move when G searched him. The cords stood out on his neck and his shoulders were bunched tighter than Joslyn had ever seen them.

"Frank, you rat," Fiona hissed at him. She took a few steps toward him as if to attack him, making him backtrack toward his computers. Joslyn wondered if she'd have the opportunity to get close enough to the computer to try to upload the virus.

However, Met moved a few steps so the gun was in her direct line of sight. "Stay where you are."

She stopped.

"I didn't invite him here, Fiona," Frank said. "He just showed up. I don't know how he found me."

"With a great deal of difficulty," Roman said with a gusty sigh. He got up and went to fling an arm around Frank's shoulders. "But I'm not complaining, because you're the next best thing. If I can't use Fiona to get Martin's money, then I'll happily use you."

"You're the one who got me into this," Frank spat at Fiona.

"I did no such thing," she retorted.

"Actually, Fiona, if you hadn't escaped, then I probably wouldn't have needed to find Frank, so it is technically your fault." Roman squeezed Frank's shoulder. "How are things going so far? Are we almost done?"

"I told you I can't just press a button, and zap! You've got money. The Bara account is protected from stuff like that."

Roman snapped his fingers. "Haven't got all day, Frank."

G had finished searching Clay and now was reaching for zip ties, probably to bind his hands together. If that happened, their chance of escaping just went into the toilet.

Clay knew it, too, because he gave Joslyn a look that she could interpret exactly. *Get ready to rumble.*

But Met still had Joslyn's gun aimed at Fiona. Joslyn didn't want to do anything that would get Fiona or Clay shot. This entire situation was out of her control. She only knew of one thing she could do.

Oh, God, she prayed, *God help us! Please help us...*

She wasn't in control, but He was. She had to remember that. She either trusted God to take care of them, or she didn't. What was it going to be?

God, I'm so scared! But I trust You.

She met Clay's eyes and gave a tiny nod. Then she caught Fiona's eyes, where a flicker of understanding passed over them.

Clay snapped his elbow back and hit G full in the face. At the same moment, Fiona dropped to the ground. Joslyn kicked at Met's gun hand, knocking it away from Fiona.

The gunshot echoed through the barn. Frank yelped and leaped backward, falling on his behind. He twisted and crawled toward a dark corner, away from the fighting.

Fiona scrambled to her feet, ran to the computer and plugged in the flash drive.

Joslyn followed up her kick with pushing the flat of her palm into Met's nose. She grabbed at the gun, but he held on tightly. With his free hand, he flailed wildly at her and his fist grazed her ear in a blow hard enough for the edges of her vision to darken. But she clung to that gun, her nails digging into the skin of his fingers.

She'd forgotten about Roman. He casually pulled a gun from inside his suit jacket and aimed it at Fiona, her back to him as she worked on one of Frank's computers.

Joslyn couldn't make her lungs and mouth

work to call Fiona's name. It was as if everything slowed down, and yet she couldn't move fast enough, she couldn't draw breath.

There was a shadow, movement, and Joslyn thought it was Frank coming out of hiding. But the figure was taller than Frank, and dressed in a dark suit. The man threw himself at Roman's gun, just as it went off.

The sound was muffled. Joslyn's stomach recoiled as she realized what that meant.

She'd been too distracted. Met jerked the gun hand away. Her hands were too slick with sweat, and she lost her grip, flying into the base of one of the metal shelves.

The impact jarred her back sharply, knocking the wind from her lungs. She twisted to keep Met in sight. She couldn't let him kick her while she was down. She'd been in that position before…

But suddenly Clay was there, tackling Met to the ground. At first Joslyn thought he must have taken care of G, but then she saw the taller man darting after him.

However, Clay grabbed a length of rebar with his good hand, and it evened the fight. He swung the metal as if he knew how to handle it, and she realized he must have had some type of training at his gym.

She got to her feet in time to see Roman stepping over the man in the dark suit where he lay on the floor.

It was Fiona's father, Martin Crowley, with red blossoming from his abdomen.

Roman raised his gun at Fiona.

Joslyn didn't think. She launched herself at Roman and the two of them landed hard on the concrete, knocking the gun away. She twisted and without trying to get up, jammed her fingers into his eyes.

He grabbed hard at her wrists, and pain shot up her arms. Then he let go of one of them and punched her in the face.

Suddenly it wasn't Roman, it was Tomas, his fists pounding into her again and again. He was out of control. There was nothing she could do to stop him.

"Joslyn!"

Clay's voice cut through the pain, broke her out of the memory. It wasn't Tomas, it was Roman. But like Tomas, he could kill her.

She wasn't about to let him do that.

Roman had risen to one knee. She lashed out with her foot and connected hard with that up-raised knee. She felt the pop of tendons.

He cried out and collapsed.

She saw the moment that Roman noticed the gun within arm's reach.

Joslyn didn't remember pulling her second weapon from her side flashbang holster. She took aim and fired, seeing Roman's wide, murderous eyes and his hand swinging his gun toward her.

There was a single gunshot. From her gun.

His hand jerked back, blood spraying from the wound.

Joslyn scrambled back out of his reach, the gun still trained on him. He was swearing and nursing his bleeding hand. She registered the sounds of Clay still fighting, but she didn't want to take her eyes off of Roman. "Fiona!"

It seemed to take a year, but suddenly Fiona had picked up Roman's gun and pointed it at him. Joslyn then got to her feet and went to where her gun had fallen to the floor. She grabbed it and shouted, "Freeze!"

The two men hesitated when they saw her with not one, but two guns pointed at them. Clay took advantage of it to knock G out cold with a blow from the rebar.

Met only looked at her in shock. "Where—?"

Thank the Lord she'd decided to wear *two* flashbang holsters. Her normal one under her arm and a tiny one on the front of her bra.

Clay knocked Met out, too, with a fist to his jaw.

Only then did Joslyn lower her weapons. Her hands were shaking. No, her entire body was shaking.

And then Clay was there, taking the two guns from her. "Are you all right?" His eyes searched her, no doubt seeing the bruises from Roman's fists.

She ignored the shaking, and all the aches in her body. She reached up, pulled his head down, and kissed him.

Clay had to get out of the barn. It smelled like blood and fried electronics and hate.

He heard a rustling behind him, the weeds being pushed aside. He smelled apricot, jasmine and cool redwoods a moment before Joslyn spoke. "Are you all right?"

"I'm—"

"Don't tell me you're fine. I heard what he said to you."

Clay turned away from her.

Back in the barn, Fiona's strangled cry had broken his and Joslyn's kiss, and suddenly Clay had been on his knees beside his stepfather's bloody figure on the floor. Fiona had been pressing her hand to the side of his abdomen.

Martin had been still but pale. As he'd seen Clay, however, his face had taken on that familiar grave look, a sneer curling his lip. "You good-for-nothing," he wheezed. "You couldn't even protect her."

Clay's entire body had suddenly filled with acid, eating at him, making his vision turn into pinpoints that only saw the disdain in his stepfather's cold eyes.

"Dad," Fiona had almost whispered.

"Clay." Joslyn's cool hand had been on his

shoulder, her voice in his ear. He'd smelled apricot, and it had soothed him. "I've called an ambulance," she'd said.

"How long will it take them to get here?" Fiona had asked.

"They said twenty-five minutes."

"I won't make it," Martin had said on a groan.

Clay had gotten up and walked away rather than saying what he really felt. He busied himself with using zipties to restrain Met and G. Richard Roman had been trying to crawl away with his busted knee and bleeding hand, but Clay caught up with him, tied his hands together and pressed a cloth to the bullet wound. Frank had disappeared entirely, which didn't surprise Clay.

Joslyn had stayed with Martin while Fiona stood in the lane and flagged down the EMT truck, leading them on the path to the barn. Clay had suspected it by now, but the paramedics had confirmed that Martin's wound wasn't serious, even though the bullet hit his side. They were inside the barn prepping him for transport right now.

Joslyn touched Clay's arm, her hand soft. He hadn't wanted to think about her kiss while he'd been in that barn, as if his stepfather's malice would taint the memory, but she had fit against him, had filled his empty places with her sweetness, comfort, acceptance. He'd found home in her arms.

"You saved me," she said. "When you called my name."

He gently caressed her cheek, which was swollen from Roman's blows. "I was frustrated because I couldn't get to you."

"I'm impressed you fought off both of those guys with a broken arm and a length of rebar."

He actually hadn't. G had managed to get hard blows to Clay's torso, shoulders and arms. G might have been avoiding hitting the cast because while he could inflict damage on Clay, striking the heavy plaster would have hurt his own hand. Either way, Clay had been able to avoid a really bad blow to his broken arm, but it still ached terribly. One of the paramedics had removed the plaster cast and said it had probably been rebroken in more places. He'd secured Clay's arm in a splint and sling, and Clay agreed to follow the truck to the ER.

The barn doors opened and the EMTs came out, carrying Martin. He complained with every step they made, and Clay wondered if maybe they were being a little rougher than usual.

Fiona followed the paramedics outside, but stopped from trailing after them through the weeds to the truck and stood beside Clay and Joslyn.

"Aren't you going with them?" Clay asked.

Fiona didn't answer for a moment. "I guess so."

It reminded him of when she was supposed to do homework and she didn't want to.

"He did take a bullet for you," he said gently. "I may have problems with him, but I'm grateful to him for that."

In the moonlight, he thought he saw tears sparkling on her lashes, but they didn't fall. "He didn't take it for me. He told me he took it so that I could survive to take over his business and continue his legacy."

"Fiona, I don't think he'd have gone to such an extreme just for his name," Joslyn said. "I think he does care about you, in his own way."

"Maybe." Then Fiona sighed and headed toward the ambulance.

"Elisabeth and Liam will be here soon," Joslyn said. "She called and said she and her FBI friends are about thirty minutes away."

"Is there enough evidence to put Richard Roman away?"

Joslyn hesitated. "I'm not sure. There's still evidence on Frank's computers to put Martin away, though."

He expected to feel some emotion at that news, but he only felt cold and flat, like coffee that had been sitting out all day. He'd overheard Martin talking to Fiona—he knew Joslyn had heard it, too. When Martin found out Clay and Joslyn were searching for Fiona and that Roman was after them, he had figured they'd be a good distraction while he tried to find Fiona on his own. He hadn't cared about the danger they were in.

Fiona had looked horrified. In combination with other things that Martin had said tonight, it seemed Fiona was having a hard time figuring out how she felt about her father.

Clay had never heard Martin be so brutally honest before. Maybe it was the wound, especially since he hadn't known how severe it was until the EMTs arrived. To Clay, who hadn't seen Martin in a while, it seemed he had become even more self-focused and driven to accomplish his own agenda. Fiona had been surprised, too, so maybe he'd gotten worse only in the two years since Fiona left LA.

Clay had been silent for too long. Joslyn touched his arm again. He had the feeling she knew what he was thinking about.

"Your past has shaped who you are, but it's not what defines you," she said. "I've done some stupid things in my past, and I'm learning how to move on. You taught me that."

"Me?" He had no idea how he'd done anything like that.

"Your strength and protectiveness made me feel brave. You made me realize not everyone's like my ex."

He touched the bruise on her cheek. "Did he hurt you?"

He thought she'd look away, but she met his eyes. "He did. It's why I froze when Roman hit me."

He couldn't imagine how awful it must have been to face that kind of terror again.

She took a deep breath. "I lost a lot because of Tomas. He killed my father, and when I ran from him, I miscarried our baby because of the fear that he'd find me."

The pain in her voice cut into him. He reached out to her, touching her face, folding her into his arms. "I'm so sorry." It seemed like such a paltry thing to say. "I wish I could do something."

"You did. I thought the counseling was going nowhere, but the past few days have shown me that I can move on. I thought I wasn't strong enough, but tonight I realized that I just wasn't trusting God enough to help me."

His arms tightened around her. "I never thought much about God before I met you. We were never close."

"What do you think of Him now?"

He cupped her face. "If God is the one giving you this strength, even after what you've been through, then I want that. I've always wanted to prove something, to find something. But all I really wanted was peace, acceptance."

"God can give you that. And I can, too."

He bent to kiss her, and there was that feeling

again, as sweet as candy, as comforting as a hand on his head. It was like sinking to the floor in front of a fireplace, or sipping tea on a back porch. He was at rest. He was enveloped. He was home.

NINETEEN

Twelve months later

Joslyn's lungs were burning as she climbed the hill. All she could see was brilliant blue sky above her, spindly trees around her on either side of the faint trail, and ahead of her, Clay's backpack like a beacon, spurring her on.

"Why again are we voluntarily going more than twenty miles away from a WiFi connection?"

He turned to grin at her. "Want some cheese with that whine?"

"You've gotten much more snarky since you started working for Shaun O'Neill." Head of security for the posh Joy Luck Life Hotel and Spa in Sonoma, Shaun had been quick to offer Clay a job as a security guard, which he'd taken.

"I don't get that from Shaun," Clay said. "I get that from Fiona. She is walking sarcasm. You should know that already."

"She's gotten worse since we were in LA."

"It's because of the trial." Fiona had agreed to testify against her father, and the FBI had indicted him on charges of money laundering.

"Is she doing okay?" Joslyn asked. She stumbled a little over a root.

"Martin still sends her letters abusing her for her betrayal." Clay's voice was grim. "I think it hurts her more than she admits. But she said she's enjoying piecing her life back together again in LA. She said she's coming up to Sonoma next week."

"Oh? What's the occasion?"

"Funny you should ask that." He'd stopped at the summit of the hill. "Come on, take a look at this."

She panted her way to the top...and then she couldn't breathe.

Unfolded in front of her was a small mountain lake. From their vantage point, she could see that it was completely surrounded by forests, without any trails that cut through the trees except for this one. The mountains of Tahoe were in the distance and reflected in the perfectly still water. Everything was silent, peaceful. It was like the seventh day of Creation, and everything was at rest.

Her breath came out long, low, filled with awe. "Oh, my."

Clay's eyes were the same glittering blue as the sky reflected in the surface of the lake. "What did I tell you? Isn't it worth the hike?"

"Oh, yes."

They made their way down the slope as the trail wended its way through tall fir trees down to the edge of the lake. Large rocks and boulders were scattered in the shallow water, and Joslyn could feel the intense cold even from a few feet away.

Everything smelled fresh and new, as if she'd never before smelled forest, or water, or rock. The air seemed purer. It filled her lungs and somehow made her feel lighter, fuller.

They were the only people here. It was amazing.

"Come on, take off your shoes." Clay shucked his hiking boots and socks and waded into the water.

Joslyn did the same and yelped at the frigid temperature, but it was refreshing. They sat on a large, flat boulder where they could see all around the lake.

"I haven't been here in years," Clay said. "I wasn't sure I could find it again, so I had to ask Bobby."

"I'm so glad you brought me."

"Let me read something to you." He took out his phone and began to read Psalm 8:

"O Lord, our Lord,
how majestic is Your name in all the earth!
You have set Your glory
above the heavens.

"When we learned about this Psalm in my

men's Bible study, I immediately thought of this place," he said. "I knew I wanted to read it out loud, here, with you."

She said, "That's perfect for this place."

He took her hand in his, and the warmth of his palm contrasted with the cold of their surroundings. "I've been learning a lot in Patrick's Bible study. He told me something once that really stuck with me. 'Love covers over a multitude of sins.'"

"That's a Bible verse," she said.

He nodded. "It's what first made me start to think seriously about God. When I was a kid, Martin always made me feel so unwanted and alone. It's not an excuse, but it spurred me to make some bad choices. I went to prison for those."

"You paid your debt." She squeezed his hand. "It's in the past."

"I was having a hard time really understanding that. I still held myself apart from people because I was sure it made me too different. But you and the O'Neills have made me feel like I belong."

"You do belong." She had a hard time remembering her life before he was in it. He'd helped her to laugh more. He'd shown her how to be adventurous—as this trip showed.

He'd helped her to stop rubbing the scar above her left eye, made from Tomas's ring.

Clay said, "Now, I want to belong to you, and I want you to belong to me."

She suddenly felt something slip onto her finger.

The ring had a round sapphire, with tiny sapphires surrounding it so that it looked like a blue flower. A bachelor's button. It made her smile.

"I hope that smile means yes," he said.

"I haven't heard a question," she retorted.

"I'm not much into speeches," he said, his face very close. "I love you, Joslyn. Will you marry me?"

She smiled, touching his face, looking into his eyes. "This smile means yes."

He kissed her, and she knew God had taken care of all of it. God would continue to take care of the two of them, to create something good out of the pain of their pasts. She only had to surrender to God. To love.

* * * * *

Dear Reader,

Thank you for joining me once again for another adventure with the O'Neill Agency! Many of you who read *Treacherous Intent* will recognize Joslyn, Elisabeth and Liam. Also, Shaun and Monica O'Neill are from *Stalker in the Shadows*.

When I wrote *Treacherous Intent*, I knew I wanted to show how Joslyn came back from the traumatic events in that book, and my hero, Clay, was the perfect person to show her that she could be a stronger person than she believed she was. I also knew that Joslyn's faith and the acceptance of the O'Neills would help Clay come to realize that he is not alone, and Jesus loves him deeply no matter what he has done in his past. I hope you've enjoyed watching them escape from explosions and fall in love.

While I love Sonoma, I also have a fondness for Lake Tahoe, and so I set part of *Gone Missing* there. It's a beautiful place to visit in the spring and summer, and of course it's a popular skiing destination in the wintertime.

You can find out more about my entire Sonoma romantic suspense series at my website, www.camytang.com.

I love to hear from readers! You can email me at camy@camytang.com or write to me at: P.O. Box 23143, San Jose CA 95123-3143. I post about knitting, my dog, knitting, tea, knitting, my husband's coffee fixation, occasional give-aways, food, oh, and did I mention my knitting obsession? Check out my Facebook page: www.facebook.com/CamyTangAuthor. I hope to see you all there!

Camy
Tang

LARGER-PRINT BOOKS!

GET 2 FREE LARGER-PRINT NOVELS PLUS 2 FREE MYSTERY GIFTS

Love Inspired®

Larger-print novels are now available...